USA TODAY BESTSELLING AUTHOR
MICHELLE HERCULES

THE PSYCHO BEFORE CHRISTMAS © 2023 by Michelle Hercules

All rights reserved.
No part of this book may be reproduced or transmitted in any form or by any means, electronic or mechanical, including photocopying, recording, or by any information storage and retrieval system without the written permission of the author, except for the use of brief quotations in a book review.

This book is a work of fiction. Names, characters, places, and incidents either are products of the author's imagination or are used fictitiously. Any resemblance to actual persons, living or dead, events, or locales is entirely coincidental.

Paperback ISBN: 978-1-959167-56-3

Deck the halls with dead bodies, fa la la la la, la la la la.
'Tis the season to be stabby, fa la la la la, la la la la.
Don we now our bloodied apparel, fa la la la la, la la la la.
Chop to bits the jerks in town, fa la la la la, la la la la.
Strike their hearts and join the chorus, fa la la la la, la la la la.
See all blazing heads before us, fa la la la la, la la la la.
Find your psycho in the chaos, fa la la la la, la la la la
Fall in love amid a feast of gory, fa la la la la, la la la la.
Merry Deathmas

This book is dedicated to everyone who had a crush on Skeet Ulrich in **Scream**.

You saw him all covered in blood with that deranged look in his eyes and thought, **Damn, that's sexy**.

playlist

SHADOWS RISE - Black Veil Brides
LOVE IS A SUICIDE - Natalie Kills
PSYCHO KILLER - Duran Duran
WE STITCH THESE WOUNDS - Black Veil Brides
BEGGIN' - Måneskin
PAIN - Four Star Mary
THE AMERICAN NIGHTMARE - Ice Nine Kills
LIKE A VILLAIN - Bad Omens
DANCING WITH THE DEVIL - Breaking Benjamin
SOMEBODY TOLD ME - Motionless In White
NIGHTMARE - Halsey
PAINT IT, BLACK - The Rolling Stones
DECK THE HALLS - Relient K

trigger warnings:

Stay away if you don't love unhinged heroes with stabbing tendencies. This novella contains dark themes, including off-page SA (not by the hero). For a more detailed trigger warning list, please check my Instagram post.

Also, be aware that the main characters aren't wired like most people, and their reactions to events and traumas aren't the norm.

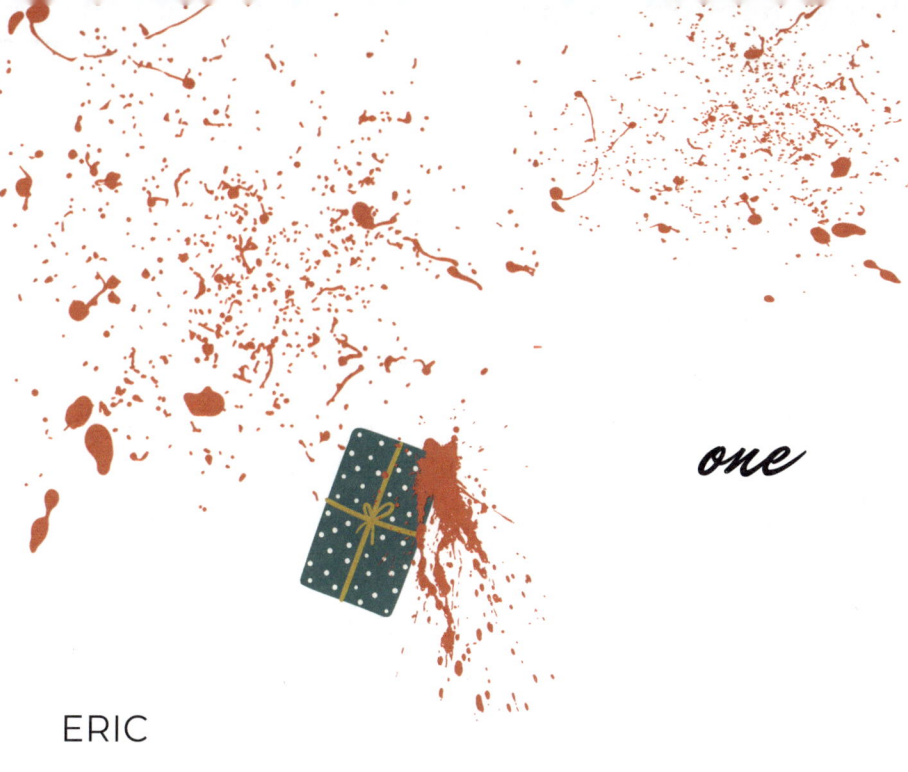

one

ERIC

It's been three months since I was forced to trade my beloved New York City for this backwater town in Oregon. It wasn't even the fact I had to start a new school for my senior year that pissed me off the most. Everyone knows everyone's business here in Stanmore, and I prefer the anonymity of a big city. I need to be able to disappear in a crowd.

My mother had to reenact a cheesy Hallmark movie and reconnect with her high school flame when she came to visit her hometown after her divorce from my dad. Keith, my stepfather, isn't terrible. He's a beloved family doctor, bland and predictable, and I guess that's what my mother needs. It helps that he's loaded and has all his hair. Mom is shallow like that. He's also a widower, so no pesky ex-wife to put a damper on Mom's marital bliss.

I'm glad she's happy. But most days, I want to crawl out of my skin. I can't carry on with my hobby here as easily as I could in the big city, and it's becoming an itch I can't scratch. If it weren't for Valerie, my stepsister, I'd probably have snapped already. We're both seniors in high school, and our folks expect us to get along. But she hates me with every fiber of her being, and her loathing soothes my dark soul.

It's noon on a Saturday, which means I just got out of bed. I should be at hockey practice, but I forgot to set my alarm. Still half-asleep, I walk into the bathroom I share with Valerie and find her there completely naked. *Jesus fucking Christ.* I'm awake now. I already knew she had a smoking hot body with all her curves, but damn, Valerie without clothes is the stuff of dreams—wet dreams.

"What the hell, Eric!" She reaches for the towel on the peg and covers herself.

"It's not my fault you didn't lock the door." I smirk. "Your extra time at the gym is paying off, sis. Your ass looks damn fine."

THE PSYCHO BEFORE CHRISTMAS

Her eyes are sparking with fury when she throws her hairbrush at me. "Get out, you perv!"

I lift my arms to protect myself, but I can't help laughing, which only makes her more furious. She tries to shove me out the door, but I'm much taller than her, and stronger, and she can't make me move. Not that she isn't strong, especially when she's incensed like that.

"I'm not kidding, Eric. Get the fuck out!" She punches my arm.

"I'll go if you give me a kiss," I taunt, knowing she'd rather kiss a frog than me.

Her pupils dilate, turning her brown eyes almost black. "Not in this lifetime or the next."

"Then I guess you'll have to wait until I'm done with the bathroom."

"I don't think so." She pinches me under the arm, making me see stars. Fuck, it brings back memories of Mom punishing me when I misbehaved in public, which happened often.

"Ouch." I step away from her, massaging the spot. "You're a psycho, you know."

She gives me a chilling smile. "You have *no* idea."

Any normal person would back the fuck off and never bother her again, but I'm far from sane, and her unhinged response makes my heart beat faster. Of course I'd have to go and get a crush on my stepsister. And I thought I was immune to clichés.

I walk out before she reads the truth in my eyes. I won't give her the upper hand by exposing my weakness. She'll use it to torture me, and not the type of torture I'm into.

I'm in the kitchen, eating breakfast, when the new doorbell sounds off its robotic rendition of "Jingle Bells." Ugh. Mom and her obsession with Christmas. It's why our house can currently be seen from outer space.

"Don't answer it. It's for me!" Valerie yells from upstairs.

"Wasn't gonna," I reply when she comes running down.

She ignores me, but I forget my cereal for a moment and watch her. She's wearing leggings and a cropped tank top that leaves nothing to the imagination. Not that I have to imagine anything now. I'm getting an über inconvenient hard-on remembering her naked body. Her smooth tanned skin, her gorgeous tits, and those legs that I wish were wrapped around my hips now.

Goddammit. Look at the fucking tent in your pants, you idiot.

It's Valerie herself who saves me from my deviant daydreaming when she dumps a huge box on the kitchen table and proceeds to open it eagerly.

"What do you have there?"

"None of your business."

"Then why are you opening it in front of me?" I arch a brow.

Her plump lips twist into a grin. "To make you eat your heart out."

I have no idea what she's talking about until she pulls out a red satin micro dress. I narrow my eyes. "What the fuck is that?"

"A dress."

"Are you sure? It looks like underwear."

She shrugs. "It's perfect for Hansen's Christmas party."

Jealousy spreads through my chest like a disease. Now I get what she meant by eating my heart out. "Hansen is a certifiable asshole."

"Is that any way to speak about your captain?"

I shove a spoonful of cereal into my mouth. Valerie is goading me, and I'm not going to fall for it. My mother insisted that I join the local hockey team so I'd make friends. Sure, I played in New York, but I was in a tier-one team. The idiots in this town are boneheads who couldn't qualify for the beer league, especially Captain Dickwad.

Valerie flattens the dress against her body and beams. "Hansen will love this."

I almost choke on my Fruit Loops. "You're not seriously thinking about hooking up with that poster child for venereal diseases, are you?"

Valerie's brows furrow. "I don't do hookups. If Hansen wants a piece of this"—she points at her body—"he needs to be my boyfriend."

I feel like I'm suffocating, drowning in my own blood, a reaction only Valerie can cause. But I can't let her see it. So I roll my eyes and say, "Good luck with that."

"I don't need luck." She sashays away with her dress, leaving the empty box in front of me.

Rage simmers low in my gut. Imagining it's Hansen's head, I punch the box across the room, creating a hole in the middle. Sadly, he's not on my list. Being a dick alone doesn't qualify him for the honor. But I'm watching him, hoping he does something that gets him there.

two

ERIC

I wasn't planning on going to Hansen's party. But like a glutton for punishment, I come to watch Valerie flirt with the douche canoe.

Bobby Smith, our goalie, is the first to see me. He lurches over, unable to walk a straight line, and stumbles into me. He's all juiced up. "Eric, what the hell, man? You missed practice."

I step back and keep him at arm's length. "Jesus Christ. How much have you had to drink already?"

"Who cares? It's a party!" He necks his beer.

"I'd stay away from open fires. You're probably highly flammable."

That reminds me, I haven't played with fire in a while. Maybe I can do some burning when I decide on a target. The thought is depressing. Back in New York, I had a mile-long list. Right now, I have only one name in the *Maybe* column. I don't believe for a second there aren't some nasty individuals in this town who need my attention. But with starting a new school, hockey, and Valerie distracting me, I haven't had time to do a proper investigation.

"Damn, Valerie is looking fiiine," Bobby says, bringing me back to the moment.

I follow his line of sight and spot her walking into the living room with Hansen glued to her side. Fucker. My hands ball into fists as I imagine all the nasty ways I can make Hansen scream like a bitch.

"You're one lucky motherfucker," Bobby keeps talking. "I'd totally tap my stepsister if she looked like that."

Valerie glances in our direction, and her eyes meet mine for a second. I make sure she notices how disgusted I am with her choice of companion. But if she cares, she doesn't show she gives a fuck. Hansen leans closer and whispers something in her ear, making her laugh.

"Hansen better not fuck around with Valerie," I grit out.

Bobby scoffs. "Yeah, like she's gonna turn him into a serious boyfriend. The man is a dog."

Maybe I should break my rules just this once. No one will truly miss that asshole. Valerie will pout for a second, then hopefully move on to someone who won't drive me to commit murder.

"Eric! You came." Carol Warner, Hansen's younger sister, beams at me.

Blonde, like her brother, and sweet to a degree that makes me wanna poke my eyes out, she's the last person I want to entertain. Mainly because she'd probably be the only one at this party who would truly mourn Hansen—and that reminds me why I have a cardinal rule.

"Hey," I say, showing the enthusiasm of a corpse watching paint dry.

"I didn't know you were coming."

"Why is that? I was invited."

She turns beet red. "I've never seen you at a party before."

Bobby throws his beefy arm around my shoulder. "Eric isn't exactly a social butterfly. But he's mean as fuck on the ice, so we forgive him for not partying hard."

"Do you want a drink?" Carol asks me.

"I don't drink."

Her eyes widen. "Never?"

"It's poison."

Tired of this conversation, I look over her head, trying to find Valerie in the crowd. I don't see her or jerkface anywhere in the living room. The house is decorated within an inch of its life with Christmas shit, and the Christmas tree in the corner might be taller than ours. If Mom finds out, she'll have a cow.

There's a group of people gathered around the dining room table doing shots—of what, I don't know. Everyone is trashed, and that grates on my nerves. Being surrounded by morons who are drunk or high is annoying as fuck when you're sober. But I don't care about joining the mindless mob. I get my thrills in a different way.

The music playing in the background becomes louder, and the song's a crowd-pleaser because cheers erupt all around me. I don't know the artist but thank fuck it isn't a Christmas song.

"Do you wanna da—" Carol starts.

"I need fresh air." I stride away from her and Bobby, getting lost in the thick of the party before I reach the back door and exit the house.

There are more people outside, hanging around a firepit. The smell of weed reaches my nose, and I spot several guys from the hockey team clustered together and passing around a joint.

One of them sees me and waves. "Yo, Eric. Join the fun, dude."

I turn around and walk away, but I still hear him say, "Weirdo."

A grin splits my face. He has no idea. It amuses me that these idiots are clueless about how much pain I could inflict on them. They're lucky I have a code.

I stick my hands in my jacket pockets and look for Valerie. Hansen's backyard borders the forest, but I doubt they went that way. It's too fucking cold. Only a psycho would draw a victim into the woods on a night like this. And Valerie isn't stupid. She'd never be lured. I glance at the crowd wistfully and sigh. I really need to find the time to make my selection.

I return to the house and decide to check the second floor. Maybe that should have been the first place I looked. I reach inside my pocket and curl my fingers around the switchblade I always carry. It isn't my weapon of choice, but it'll do in a pinch.

Jesus, Eric. You can't fillet Hansen just because Valerie might be screwing him.

Well, I *could*, but I'd never be dumb enough to do it in a house full of people. Too many witnesses tying me to the murder scene. Plus, Valerie would see the whole thing. I couldn't bring myself to kill her too. This isn't a slasher movie, and I don't plan on getting arrested... ever.

I let go of the switchblade before I start opening doors. One of the rooms is occupied, but I don't recognize the couple. They're so busy fucking they don't even notice me. I leave the door open just for kicks.

All the other rooms I open are empty, including the one that can only belong to Hansen. Where the hell are they?

three

ERIC

It's past midnight when I finally hear Valerie stomp up the stairs and bang her bedroom door shut. Mom and Keith are still at the mayor's Christmas party.

I want to know where the hell she's been, so I barge into her room without knocking. She jumps and turns around, holding her dress in place. Both spaghetti straps are hanging loose on the sides as if someone tore them off.

My blood runs cold. *Hansen.*

Valerie should have yelled at me already for

invading her privacy, but she keeps staring with eyes as round as saucers while her breath comes out in bursts.

I shorten the distance between us, and then I notice dried blood on her lower lip from a small cut and a bruise on her neck in the shape of a hand.

"Who did this to you?" I ask in a cold and tight voice, already knowing the answer.

She steps back. "Nobody."

"Don't bullshit me, Valerie. It was Hansen, wasn't it?"

Her eyes harden. "I said it was nobody. Leave it alone, Eric."

Fuck. If she seemed frightened, I could believe she didn't want to tell me out of fear. But her eyes are flashing with anger, and it's aimed at me. My stomach coils tight, making me sick. She can't possibly be in love with that scumbag.

"Why are you protecting him?"

"I'm not protecting anyone," she grits out.

"Then tell me how you busted your lip and why your brand-new dress is destroyed."

She chuckles, but her eyes remain cold. "Maybe I like it rough. Have you thought of that?"

Take a knife and plunge it into my heart, why don't you?

I don't buy her bullshit though. Hansen hurt her, and that's all I need to know. But I can't simply leave, so I step closer and run my fingers down her arm. "If you truly liked it rough, you wouldn't have gone to Hansen, Val. You would have come to me."

She gasps, and her eyes widen. God, even with the fury of a raging fire burning through my veins, I want to kiss her. For the first time, she's looking at me as if she's considering the possibility that I could be more than her stepbrother. The space between us seems to crackle with electricity. I don't make a move, waiting for Valerie to decide.

The sound of the front door opening breaks the spell. Our parents are home. I step back and run my fingers through my long bangs to try to dispel the fog of lust that almost made me cross a line. Then I spin around and walk out of her room.

I might be lacking a soul, but I don't take advantage of girls. Something bad happened to Valerie, and I intend to find out how bad. I'll make sure Hansen sings before I'm done with him.

VALERIE

I let out a breath of relief when Eric leaves me alone. He caught me having a weak moment while I was still reeling from what happened with Hansen, and I hate that. But then he said the first real thing to me since he came into my life.

He's always flirted with me but never seriously. He does it to get on my nerves. Tonight was different. I could see the desire blazing in his eyes, and I almost caved despite what happened at the party. I'm not like most people. I don't react the same way to bad things as most of the population does. What Hansen did was the most extreme shit that's happened to me. A different girl would be curled up in a corner, crying herself senseless, and be broken for a very long time. Not me.

I've had a crush on Eric ever since I met him. How could I not? Those baby-blue eyes that always burn with intensity, those lips that can curl in the most wicked smile, and a face that belongs on the cover of a magazine. But besides his looks, it's the disdain he seems to have for humanity in general and his dark sense of humor that draw me to him. He's been a pest since he moved in, though, so I focus on that and try to ignore my attraction to him.

If our folks hadn't arrived home when they did, I might have crossed the line with him. Not only to fulfill a fantasy but also to eradicate the memory of Hansen's touch. Thinking about him fills me with rage. My body starts to shake, and I want to break things. I curl my hands into fists, digging my long nails into my palms until it hurts. Then I take deep breaths, willing my pulse to slow down. I can't act on impulse. Revenge is best served cold, and Hansen will get what's coming to him.

I take off my ruined dress and toss it in the trash. I want to burn it, but I'll do that later. First, I need a scalding-hot shower. My skin burns when the jets hit me, but I endure the pain until I get used to it. I wash myself twice, and then I get ready in an all-black ensemble that reflects my mood. My shoulder-length hair will have to dry naturally. I don't want to wake my father by blow-drying it. I need something from his office.

He keeps pharmaceutical samples locked in a cabinet, but I made a copy of the key a long time ago. I've been stealing shit from him for years. I love to experiment with chemicals, especially ones that can kill without a trace. I have some vials of poison in my room already, but none of them will do. They kill too quickly, and I want Hansen to suffer for what he did to me. He fucked with the wrong girl.

four

ERIC

I usually plan my kills better. Preparation and research are half the fun, after all. But there's no fucking chance I'll wait to make that motherfucker pay. Hansen hurt Valerie, and he doesn't deserve to live to see another day.

Before I return to his house, I need my tools. When I moved to Stanmore, I had to find a place to hide them. Keeping my stash in the house wasn't an option. But one of the advantages of living in the boonies is that there isn't a shortage of woodland around. My hiding spot is a minute's drive from Keith's house, but I cycle there. No car engine noises to draw attention. Plus, that way, no one can see my license plate and put me at the scene.

I created a miniature bunker in the middle of the forest. It's a sixty-by-sixty-inch hole that fits the metal box with a hatch that I commissioned. To keep it hidden, all I have to do is cover it with dirt.

Tonight, the snow is thick, but I marked the spot. It's in front of a tall tree that I carved with the initials *E* and *V*, surrounded by a heart. When I did it, it was a joke and less suspicious than using a generic *X*. But now the joke is on me because I ended up falling for Valerie in the end.

I clear the snow from the top and open my treasure box. A smile blossoms on my lips. I've missed my toys. I take out my favorite weapon in the collection, a bowie knife with a serrated blade that cuts through muscle and bone as if they're butter. It's a fucking dream.

I set it aside and peruse my assortment of masks. I like variety. I kill to rid the world of monsters, not to become famous. It's also fun and fulfilling, and that's all the reward I need.

I'm sure there are still people at Hansen's house, so I have to take extra precautions to not be recognized. I've been dying to don the scary Santa mask I wore once to a Halloween party last year, and tonight, it fits the theme perfectly.

Besides my weapons in the box, I have a change of clothes—all black—and gloves. They'll be disposed of once I'm done. It's the perfect night for a bonfire.

I shrug off my coat and put the black attire over my clothes because, one, it's fucking cold and I don't want to undress in the middle of the forest, and two, I want to disguise my body type in case there are witnesses. The bulkier I look, the better.

I stab at the air, testing my outfit to make sure it doesn't hinder my movements. The exercises make my blood pump faster, and a thrill of excitement courses down my back. It's been too long since my last kill.

Satisfied with my getup, I shove the mask and the knife into my backpack and shut and lock the box. Then I cover the lid again with dirt and snow. I also make sure to erase my footprints up to the tree. This takes a bit of time, but I can't risk anyone finding my hiding spot.

On the way to Hansen's house, I put in my AirPods and listen to Christmas songs. When "Deck the Halls" plays, I mouth the words. Nothing gets me jollier than the prospect of slashing a motherfucker to bits. But then I remember why Hansen found himself on my hit list, and my enthusiasm wilts to nothing. I wanted him to do something awful, so I'd have the excuse to end him, but I didn't want Valerie to be his victim.

I turn off the music. I'm no longer in the mood for it. Five minutes later, I pass by Hansen's house. As I predicted, there are still people there. That means his parents must still be at the mayor's party. Mark Warner, Hansen's father, is a bigshot in town and he never misses those parties. I keep going until I find a good spot to hide my bike and my backpack.

The knife and mask I hide in a jacket pocket during the walk back to Hansen's party. I keep to the shadows, avoiding the glow of Christmas decorations. Hansen lives in an upscale neighborhood; I don't want to catch the attention of a nosy neighbor who thinks I'm a burglar.

Animated voices reach my ears. I veer for the back of the house and hide in the bushes surrounding the property. There aren't too many people left, just two I can see, Bobby and Doug, another guy on the team. Both are completely trashed.

The back door opens, and Hansen walks out, holding a bottle of whiskey in one hand and a joint in the other. A drunk and a junkie. I sneer. What did Valerie see in this loser?

He can barely walk straight and almost falls on top of Bobby, who's sitting in a lawn chair.

"Dude, watch where you're going." Bobby laughs then snatches the whiskey from Hansen.

Like he needs more alcohol. Dumbass.

"Shut up."

"Where did Valerie go?" Doug asks.

Hansen takes a hit of his joint, then asks, "Why? Do you wanna fuck that bitch too?"

My nostrils flare, and my hand finds the hilt of my knife. But I've been doing this for a while. I know how to control my temper and wait for the perfect moment to strike.

"I wouldn't pass up that chance. Are you offering?" Doug chuckles.

Keep talking, asshole, I might make tonight a two-for-one special.

Hansen shrugs. "Be my guest. She was a lousy fuck anyway. But I showed her nobody says no to me."

Bobby and Doug laugh, but I keep my attention on Hansen.

After ten minutes or so, Bobby gets up from his chair and stretches. "Man, I'm gonna crash on your couch if you don't mind."

"Whatever."

Doug stands too. "Yeah, I'm beat. I gotta sleep."

"You can both crash here, but no screwing around. If I catch you two losers fucking, I'll cut your dicks off."

"Fuck off, Hansen. I'm not a homo," Doug retorts.

"Yeah, yeah. Whatever."

They disappear inside the house, leaving Hansen alone. I wait another minute to make sure Bobby and Doug aren't coming back, then I put on the mask.

Hansen gets up from his chair and almost falls over. Then he staggers toward the bushes, close to my hiding spot, and unzips his pants. It's my cue to move.

While he's pissing, I walk around the bushes and approach him from behind, not bothering to be stealthy. I want him to hear my approach.

Hansen turns his face to the side and says, "I'm not letting you sleep in my room."

"I don't want to sleep in your room, you piece of shit," I say in a low voice so he can't recognize it.

He turns around, still holding his dick. "Who the fuck are you, creep?"

"What's the matter, Hansen? It's me, Santa. I came to deliver your gift."

I strike faster than Hansen can react and off goes his dick. He screams, but the sound is cut short by the slash to his throat. That'll kill him in seconds, but I'm far from satisfied. He drops to the ground, clutching his neck and gasping for air. His eyes are round with fear and pain. Not enough of either though.

I drop to my knees next to his body and stab him

over and over again, avoiding making other fatal wounds. I want to make him suffer for as long as possible. Before his eyes dim forever, I find his severed dick on the ground and shove it in his mouth.

"Merry Deathmas, motherfucker."

five

VALERIE

I didn't sleep much last night, which accounts for me waking up later than usual. I'm usually up before dawn, even on weekends. I'm on the track team, and I have to practice come rain or shine. But I'm taking a day off today. There's a lot to do, and I need to focus on revenge, or I'll have too much time to dwell on what happened to me. I refuse to be the victim who blames herself for the actions of others. I never imagined Hansen could be such a monster. He hides his true nature well.

I'll make sure I'm the last girl he ever hurts.

I have to wear a turtleneck sweater to hide the

bruise that mongrel left on my neck. Unfortunately, I can't hide my busted lip. I'd have more bruises if I'd fought him harder, but I knew I couldn't stop him and no help would be coming. He took me to his favorite spot, a cabin in the woods behind his parents' property. I thought it was romantic, but I soon found out he just wanted to make sure no one would hear me scream. I chose to disconnect while he had his fun with me because I knew he'd get more pleasure if I fought him. I doubt any person in that situation would have made that cold decision, but it was easier knowing he'd pay for it sooner rather than later. I can't wait to watch his face as he dies slowly.

It's already past nine, and everyone in the house is up, including Eric. What's surreal is that he's sitting at the dining room table having breakfast with his mother and my father. He rarely eats meals with the family.

Dad glances at me, and I notice a strange gleam in his eyes, almost as if he knows what happened to me. "Good morning, sweetheart. You slept in."

I turn to Eric. If he opened his big mouth, he'll be sorry. I could never kill him, but I could give him something that'd make him shit for days.

His eyes meet mine, bluer than ever, sending a frisson of excitement down my spine. His gaze feels different today, more intense, more... *hypnotic*. I get a funny feeling in my stomach, as if butterflies were fluttering inside me while high on speed. How in the world did I ever think Hansen could be a substitute for Eric?

"Val?" Dad asks again.

I blink fast, turning to him. "Yeah. I was tired." He flattens his lips and his brows furrow. That's Dad's signature look when he's troubled. "Did something happen?"

"I'm afraid so, honey," Theresa replies. Always super polished; she looks a bit ragged this morning. Her bleached blonde hair isn't perfectly styled, and she's not wearing any makeup, allowing me to see that she isn't as young as she wants to be.

I pull up a chair and wait for one of them to fill me in. They look like they're about to tell me someone died. I'd be concerned if there were anyone left in my family besides my father and now Theresa and Eric. But my mother is dead, and so are my grandparents on both sides. I don't have any uncles or aunts, and any cousins I might have are too many times removed for me to care.

"Okay, what is it?"

Dad lets out a heavy sigh, but it's Eric who answers, "Hansen is dead."

I whip my face toward him. "*What?*"

"Eric, he was your friend. You sound like you don't care." Theresa chides him.

"First of all, he wasn't my friend. And secondly, will beating around the bush make him less dead?" He arches a brow.

I'm spiraling, and black dots appear in my line of vision. Hansen can't be dead... not yet. I need to be the one to end him. "How did he die?"

Dad's face seems to grow paler. "He was... murdered."

Hell to the fucking no. Someone beat me to it? I grab a piece of bread and start to rip it apart. I need to destroy something, and since I can't start breaking plates without being committed, the bread it is. "How?"

"You don't want to know all the gruesome details, honey," Theresa replies, her eyes full of pity.

I don't need your pity, lady. I need Hansen to be alive so I can kill him.

"We received a call from the sheriff last night. They want your statement and Eric's, but you were asleep, and I didn't want to wake you with the bad news," Dad continues.

I push away from the table and stand. "I need a moment alone."

ERIC

I watch Valerie run up the stairs and lose my appetite. I didn't expect her to react like that to the news of Hansen's demise. Even after what he did to her, she still cares about that asshole? I'm livid and jealous as fuck. The feeling is so overwhelming that it vanquishes my good mood. The high after a kill usually lasts a couple weeks. Considering I had a personal vendetta against Hansen, I expected the euphoria to last longer. Now it's gone.

I stand. "I'm gonna check on Val."

Keith's eyes soften, and gratitude shines in them. "You do that, son."

Man, he was happy to pass on the task. He doesn't seem to like dealing with feelings. It makes me wonder how he delivers bad news to his patients.

I take the stairs two steps at a time, but when I stop in front of Valerie's door, I stop and knock. "Val, can I come in?"

"Go away, Eric."

Yeah, like that's gonna happen.

I open the door—in this house, none of them have locks, save for the bathrooms. Keith is weird like that.

"I told you to go away," she says from her desk, but she keeps staring out the window.

Valerie's room is immaculate but cozy. The walls are a soft peach color, the duvet white, and there are so many pastel-colored pillows on her bed that they take up a third of the mattress. The decor is completely at odds with her black-cat personality.

Ignoring her request, I walk in and close the door behind me. "Are you okay?"

She swivels in her chair and glares at me. "You never listen, do you?"

At least she's not crying over Hansen.

"No. You should know that by now. But seriously, Val. Are you okay?"

She lets out a shuddering breath. "No. I'm not okay. Hansen is dead."

I cross my arms. "No great loss there if you ask me. What did you ever see in him?"

Maybe now's not the time to try to understand what attracted Valerie to that scumbag in the first place. After learning what he did to her, I expected her to be relieved he's worm food.

Her eyes widen. "Why do you care?"

"Morbid curiosity, I guess." I shrug.

She doesn't answer, but she holds my stare. I wish I could read her mind. My pulse is racing, but my heart feels tight like it's being squeezed by a boa constrictor. I never realized how hard I'd fallen for Valerie until this moment. I'm jealous of a dead man.

Suddenly, she jumps from the chair and strides toward me. I have no idea what her intentions are, but there's a storm brewing in her dark eyes. I uncross my arms and tense, not knowing if I'm about to get punched in the throat or shoved out of her room.

I don't expect Valerie to curl her fingers into my T-shirt and yank me to her. Her soft lips slant over mine, and it's like I've been hit by lightning. All my nerve endings short-circuit. My surprise lasts only a second before my arms circle her waist and I deepen the kiss she started. Her tongue is sweet and spicy, and it tastes better than I could have ever imagined. I'm unraveling, and I don't care why she's kissing me.

Pulling her body flush to mine, I release her mouth and trail open kisses down her chin and neck. She's wearing a turtleneck sweater, so I push the fabric down to have access to her skin. Fury surges within me when I see the bruise Hansen gave her. It's darker now. I regret I didn't make him suffer more.

Gasping, Valerie throws her head back, stretching her neck as an offering to me. "Don't stop, Eric. I want your mouth on me."

I grab her chin and force her to look into my eyes. "Where, kitty cat?"

Her eyes focus on mine, burning with intensity. "Everywhere."

The electric sparks in her stare set me ablaze. My heart beats violently inside my chest as if trying to escape. I kiss her again, hard and fast, and it's a battle between tongues and teeth. Valerie's hands find my hair, and then she yanks at the strands but not to pull me off her. The pain makes my already rock-hard cock even harder. I'm fucking glad I'm still wearing sweatpants and no underwear.

I ease off and pick her up, digging my fingers into her sweet ass. She wraps her legs around my hips, pressing her pussy against my erection. I gyrate her hips, causing much-needed friction between our bodies. "Do you feel that, kitty cat?"

"Yes," she hisses, then kisses my neck, sucking it hard.

God, my girl is feral, and I love it.

I turn to her bed and drop her on the edge of the mattress. Looking into my eyes, she breathes hard now, and her lips are already swollen from my kisses. I don't make a move, trying to read her mind again. Maybe I'm waiting for her to snap out of the moment and kick me out of her room after all. But instead, she yanks my pants down, freeing my cock.

Her gaze drops to my erection, then she curls her

fingers around the base. "I guess your Big Dick Energy is justified."

"Did you have any doubt?" I push her sharp bangs back, then twist a lock of her silky hair around my fist.

"Not really." She meets my stare again and runs her tongue from my balls to the head. A groan escapes my mouth, and I hold her hair tighter.

"Are you going to suck it, or are you determined to only tease?"

"What if I only want to tease?"

I don't answer right away, knowing this is a test.

"Then you can tease me all you want, kitty cat. Whatever you need, I'm here for you."

Her eyes widen, and for a second, I catch a glimpse of vulnerability. She releases my cock and scooches back. "I think I'd rather you eat me out first."

Immediate relief follows. I was totally expecting to be kicked out. My lips split into a grin. "As you wish. But I need to see those lovely tits first. Ugly sweater off."

She grabs the hem and peels her top off. She's not wearing a bra. Her breasts are as delectable as I remember, full and begging to be worshipped. My mouth is already watering. I take my pants off and then roll Valerie's leggings down her legs too.

"If I'm going to be completely naked, you need to get rid of all your clothes too," she says.

My T-shirt disappears in the blink of an eye, and I get the satisfaction of watching Valerie ogling me. She swallows hard and when her eyes return to my face, they're shining with undiluted desire. I kneel between her legs and bring my face inches from her flat stomach. She leans back, leaning on her forearms, and her chest rises and falls fast. Keeping eye contact, I run my tongue across her belly just above her underwear's elastic band. Her white cotton panties are simple, but they're sexy as hell to me.

"Should I stop?"

Her brows furrow. "If you do, I'll hurt you."

I chuckle. "Such violence."

"You have no idea."

"I'd love to see it, but not today." I pull her panties down and have to control my emotions for a moment. She's bruised there too. Too bad I can't kill that scumbag again. I focus on how smooth her pussy is and how it's glistening, ready for me. "You're so wet for me already, Val. I love it."

I lick her clit slowly so I can savor her taste properly, but she's more delicious than I could have imagined, and keeping my pace slow is impossible. I flick my tongue left and right while massaging the area just above her clit. Valerie moans like the kitten she is, and that spurs me on. I spread her legs wider and suck her clit into my mouth hard, making her hips buckle.

She threads her fingers through my hair and whispers, "I need more, Eric. I need you inside of me."

I pull back and look at her. "Are you sure?"

Even though her eyes are hooded, I read determination in them. "I'm sure. I need it, Eric. Please."

Fury makes my body shake. Fuck Hansen all the way to hell. I have to work hard to keep it in check, and not let her see it. I know Valerie is using me to forget what that fucker did to her. I have no illusions here. She wouldn't suddenly develop feelings for me. But I killed for her, fucking her into oblivion is a no-brainer.

"Where do you keep your condoms?"

"First drawer in the nightstand."

I find a few wrappers and take one out. Valerie keeps watching me with fire in her eyes, her determination unwavering. I roll the condom down my shaft then return to my spot between her legs, grabbing her thighs. "How do you want it, kitty cat? Slow and tender or fast and hard?"

"I told you already. I like it rough. I want you to cover all my bruises with the ones you make."

My heart skips a beat. "I'll make sure of that, kitty

cat." I lift her hips off the mattress and, with one hard thrust, sheath myself in her.

She gasps, but I don't stop. I understand her need to feel this pain because it's on her own terms. It's her choice. I pull back almost all the way, only to slam back into her again. She's so slick that it makes it easy to increase my pace. The bed starts to make an awful noise as the headboard bangs against the wall. The possibility of getting caught by our parents adds another layer of thrill. My balls are getting tight and heavy, but I'm not coming until Valerie does. I fuck her harder while pressing my thumb against her clit.

"Fuck, Eric. That feels so good. Don't stop."

"Come for me, Val. I know you're close. You're already milking my cock so good."

She arches her back, curling her fingers around the duvet. "Yes, I'm coming, oh fuck, I'm coming!"

I watch her unravel in front of me, and it's a thing of beauty. Her flushed cheeks, the thin layer of perspiration across her forehead, and her delirious gaze—it's almost enough to make me lose control. *Almost.* I can give her another orgasm before she destroys me too.

"I can make it even better." I lift both her legs and hold them close together against my chest. Tendrils of desire curl around the base of my spine, giving me goose bumps. To keep from coming too soon, I clench my butt cheeks. This new angle feels so fucking good. She's even tighter like this.

"Eric.... what are you doing to me?" she murmurs.

"What you asked me to, kitty cat. I'm branding you."

"Dammit. You're stretching me so good. I can't stand it." She begins to close her eyes, but I'm not having it.

"Eyes on me, gorgeous. See what you do to me."

She whimpers, and then tremors run through her body. She's coming again, but this time, she's riding the wave quietly—or as quietly as she can. My control snaps, and I reach the point of no return. My cock throbs inside her tight pussy while the orgasm runs me over like an eighteen-wheeler truck.

I part her legs and set them down on the mattress so I can lean forward and claim her lips again. I kiss her until the shakes wreaking havoc on my body subside, and her body goes slack under mine. My breathing is completely out of whack. While I wait for my pulse to return to normal, I hide my face in the crook of her neck and take my fill of her sweet scent. I wish I could stay inside her longer, but reality comes knocking—well, my mother comes knocking.

"Valerie? Can I come in?"

I lean back and look over my shoulder, expecting

my mother to walk in at any second and catch me buried deep inside Valerie.

"No. I just got out of the shower," she answers.

"Oh, okay. Well, the sheriff called again. He wants to take your statement this morning."

I glance at Valerie and find her looking at me as if I'm nuts. Then she mouths, *Get off me.*

Right. The fun is over. We're back to the status quo. But I don't regret giving Valerie two mind-blowing orgasms. Anything to make her forget that deep shit.

six

VALERIE – *ONE YEAR LATER*

I've been back home for a week and have had to endure Theresa's obsession with Christmas by myself. Dad is as busy as ever with his practice, and Eric has yet to show his face in Stanmore. He must be having way too much fun in New York to bother coming home. The thought is bitter.

I don't actually know if that's the case. Maybe he's just avoiding me for as long as he can. I'll never know. He shut down when I told him there wouldn't be a repeat of our hookup. He never asked for a reason, so I took his reaction to mean he didn't want a repeat anyway.

That hurt.

He doesn't know that after he escaped my room using our shared bathroom, Theresa came in and told me without preamble that a relationship between Eric and me would destroy her marriage with my dad. He wouldn't accept it. She wasn't wrong. Dad is traditional to a fault, plus in this small town, the scandal would probably ruin his practice. As much as I think Theresa is over the top, she makes my father happy. I couldn't ruin his happiness on the off chance Eric might like me. After that morning, my relationship with him turned ice cold and more antagonizing than ever. Hate is a great mask.

But I had other things to keep me distracted—Hansen's gruesome murder investigation. I needed to know who his killer was so I could make them pay for denying me my revenge. Sadly, Stanmore's Sheriff's Department never solved the crime. All they had was the unreliable testimony of Bobby Smith, who swore Santa killed Hansen.

The name Killer Santa was born, and the local newspaper ran with that story for months. Interest in the case eventually died out, but with the anniversary of Hansen's murder just around the corner, people are talking about Killer Santa again. There's a memorial mass for him tomorrow at church. It's the last place I want to be, but if I don't show up, people will talk. The entire town will be there.

"Val, honey. Did you find the silver tinsel?" Theresa calls from downstairs.

I'm helping her decorate the living room, and she seems to have misplaced the tinsel she bought last week. The house should have been decked out already, but she decided to change the color scheme of the decor. *Last week.*

"Not yet," I yell back. "Are you sure you put the box in your closet?"

"Ugh. I don't know. Check Eric's room. I might have put it in *his* closet."

Great. Like I really want to go in his room. Not that I never snooped around his bedroom before, but I've avoided going near it since I got home from college. I don't want any reminder that I haven't been able to extract the pest from my heart.

Annoyed that Theresa is forcing me into his domain, I clench my teeth and go look for the damn tinsel box. Eric's closet is pretty sparse. He took most of his clothes when he started school at Clayton U in New York City. Not that he had many to begin with. Ever since I've known him, he's stuck to his basic dark jeans, T-shirts, and his black leather jacket. Whenever it gets

THE PSYCHO BEFORE CHRISTMAS

super cold, he adds a few more layers and wears a thicker coat.

The closet still smells like him though, a mix of nutmeg, cedar, mandarin orange, and lemon. It's intoxicating, just like him. The scent brings back the memory of us being together that I shoved into a dark corner of my mind. I can almost feel the heat of his skin against mine and the way he unraveled me with his tongue. Luckily, I find the box Theresa needs right away. I drop into a crouch to pick it up, and that's when I sense I'm no longer alone... and it's not my stepmom standing behind me.

"What are you doing in my closet, Val?"

I unfurl from my crouch slowly, holding the box. I need the shield when I turn to face him. He's standing under the doorframe, taking up most of the space with his six-foot-three-inch height. His shoulders look wider than I remember. But his gorgeous face and his intense blue eyes are what makes my knees weak.

I lift my chin in defiance, narrowing my eyes. "Your mother sent me to get the tinsel box."

He arches a brow, and the corners of his mouth curl upward into a crooked grin. "What's that box doing in my closet?"

"Ask her." I take a step forward, but Eric is still blocking the exit. "Are you gonna move or what?"

Still smirking, he takes a sidestep, but as I walk past him, he grabs my arm. "What? I don't get a hug from you?"

I frown. "Why do you need a hug?"

"'Cause I haven't seen you in months, Val, and we're family."

Family. The word makes me sick when I associate it with Eric. It's thanks to that notion that we can't be together—not that *he* wants that. He probably considers last year's hookup a favor, nothing more.

"Whatever. Hug your mother." I try to yank my arm free, but Eric holds me tighter.

"I already did. I want a hug from *you.*"

"You're not getting a hug from me. Now let go."

His gaze hardens, and instead of releasing my arm, he pulls me closer and brings his mouth to my ear. "I've missed you, Val. You know what date tomorrow is, right?"

His warm breath against my skin makes me lightheaded. God, I want him to kiss me so desperately that it's a little scary.

"Yes," I whisper. "Hansen's murder anniversary."

"You know that's not what I meant." He licks my neck, turning my body into jelly. Desire quickly spreads through me, and I close my eyes.

"Valerie, did you find the box?" Theresa asks from

the hallway.

Eric releases my arm and steps away. When his mother walks in, there's a safe distance between us, but she still studies us as if she knows exactly what we've been up to.

"I got the box," I reply.

"Good. Come downstairs and let Eric rest."

"I'm not tired. I can help decorate." He looks at me, and my face heats. Shit. I hope his mother doesn't notice.

Theresa arches a brow. "You? Decorate the house for Christmas?"

"Why not?"

I can't be near Eric while my hormones are all over the place. I snort. "Hell no. You'll end up ruining everything."

His expression becomes serious. "I'll just chop some wood then."

"That's a great idea, sweetheart," Theresa pipes up, then turns to me. "Come on, Val. There's so much work left to do."

I shouldn't, but I can't resist looking over my shoulder as I walk out of Eric's room. There's a glint of something deranged in his eyes now, and it makes my breath catch but not out of fear. It's excitement that's making my blood rush faster through my veins.

seven

ERIC

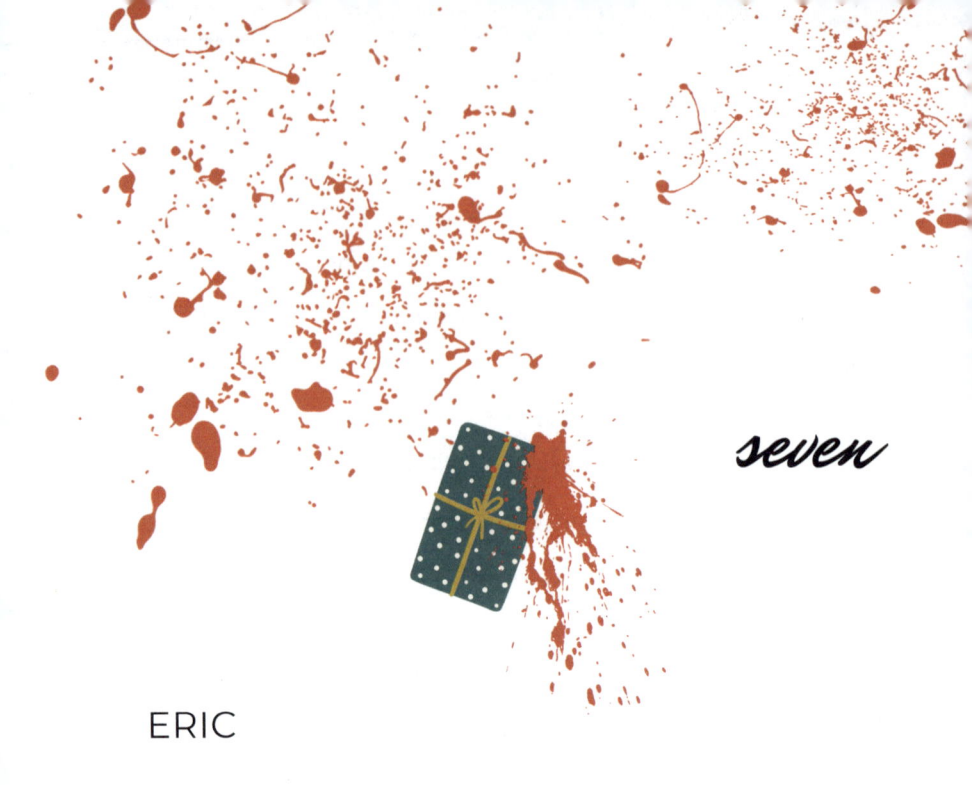

I swore to myself I wouldn't start things with Valerie again. She made it crystal clear last year she wanted nothing more to do with me. I was resigned that she would never be mine, and yet I made arrangements to be close to her again just the same by transferring to Hawthorne University for the upcoming spring semester. It was all set up. I knew I wouldn't be able to give up the pain of being near her and not having her. It was almost as good as *having* her. I'd have enrolled at Hawthorne U in the first place, but I had unfinished business in New York City. There were some assholes on my list that had to go.

But the moment I saw her after all these months apart, I forgot all about my vow. The need to possess every part of her being returned with a vengeance. Never mind that she doesn't want anything to do with me.

Chopping wood sounds like the perfect distraction, and it's also good practice. I still prefer my bowie knife, but lately, I've had a couple kills where I switched to an axe. It requires more strength, so I've been hitting the gym more often to get the job done with better precision.

I thought being back in New York City would cure me of my obsession with Valerie. Being busy with school, the hockey team, and my long list of targets should have kept my mind from wandering to her. No such luck.

It takes an hour to finish my chore, and by the time I return to the house, Mom and Valerie have finished putting the final touches on the decor. I'm surprised Mom was still busy with that. She starts putting Christmas decorations up as soon as Thanksgiving is over.

Valerie is sitting at the kitchen table, distracted by her iPad, and Mom is baking Christmas cookies. The smell makes my mouth water and my stomach rumble.

"I'm all done," I announce, loud enough to get

Valerie's attention. She doesn't lift her gaze from her screen, but her brows furrow.

"Good. Wash your hands, and you can have some of the first batch of cookies," Mom replies, but I keep staring at Valerie.

"What are you reading that's making you that angry, sis? Your horoscope?"

"Bite me, Eric," she snaps.

Oh, the retort that's on the tip of my tongue. She totally teed it up for me, but I can't say it in front of my mother.

Mom steps closer and whispers, "Valerie is probably reading another article about Killer Santa. The news started focusing on that again with… you know."

That vanquishes my good mood. "I can't believe you're still mourning Hansen," I tell Valerie.

She snaps her face up. "Mourning that loser? Are you nuts?"

Okay, I wasn't expecting that answer and neither was my mother, judging by how her eyes widen.

"Why are you upset about those articles then?" I ask.

"Because it's a reminder of how worthless the Sheriff's Department is. How could they not catch Hansen's killer?"

Uneasiness settles in the pit of my stomach. I don't

regret killing that motherfucker, but what if Valerie finds out it was me? Will she rat me out? I'd never silence her permanently to avoid spending the rest of my life in prison, but my biggest fear is having her recoil from me in disgust. I'm a deranged psycho, after all. It doesn't matter that I only kill monsters. Most people would run away.

"His killer is probably long gone," I say.

She holds my stare, and I can almost hear the gears in her head working at full speed. "Or maybe the killer is closer than we think."

I shove a cookie in my mouth, earning a slap on the arm from my mother. "You didn't wash your hands."

"Sowwy mowm," I reply with my mouth full.

Valerie sneers. "You're a pig."

I open my mouth wide, showing my chewed food to her. Her face twists into a scowl.

"Eric. Stop that. And go shower. Your father will be home soon, and I'd like us to have a proper family meal."

I open my mouth to argue that Keith isn't my father but think better of it. He always insists that I think of him as such, and I don't want to hurt my mother's feelings. Besides, he's far better than my old man, who doesn't give a fuck if I'm dead or alive. He writes a fat check every month, and that's the extent of his fatherly duties. He's too busy being a shark on Wall Street, after all.

On my way to the stairs, I glance at Valerie again. She's staring at me in a peculiar way, almost as if she wants to tell me something but can't.

"Val, dear, would you like a cookie?" Mom asks, drawing her attention.

"Sure."

I shake my head. I must be imagining things. I decide then that I'm going on a recon mission after dinner. Maybe I can catch someone up to no good. It'd be fun if I got to wear my Santa mask again. That'd set the town in a panic. A serial killer who strikes only around Christmastime. I chuckle. Now that's what I call a jolly idea.

🔪🔪🔪

VALERIE

Dinner was painful. Eric sat across from me and stared at me the entire time. I had to pretend I didn't notice his searing gaze, especially in front of Theresa. Ever since she found out I screwed her son, she's been watching us like a hawk. She never told me how she found out, but my father remains in the dark.

Thankfully, dinner is over, and I can hide in the safety of my room—that is if Eric doesn't decide to sneak in to torture me more. I lie in bed and hope he'll come, but when it gets late and he doesn't show up, I'm disappointed. *What did you expect, Valerie? You put him in the icebox for a year.*

I should try to get some sleep, but the sound of a door opening in the hallway makes me alert. I don't hear footsteps, so whoever is out there is trying to be stealthy. My heart skips a beat, thinking that it's Eric finally coming here, but my door never opens. What the hell!

I get out of bed and, on soft feet, walk to my door. There's no one in the hallway now, which means they already made it downstairs. I'm almost certain Eric's the one sneaking around the house this late. I put on my fuzzy slippers and go down. Thanks to all the Christmas lights, I can see where I'm going without needing to turn on the main lights. There's no one in the kitchen—I thought perhaps he came down for a midnight snack. But then I notice light pouring through the cracks of the garage door.

He's sneaking out!

Maybe he's going to meet a hookup. Jealousy makes me see red. I know it's crazy. Eric isn't my boyfriend, but hell, the idea that he might have someone in town makes me sick to my stomach. I march to the door and open it wide just in time to see Eric steering his bicycle toward the garage side door.

He's dressed to go out in his puffy black coat, beanie, and scarf. He freezes and looks at me. "Valerie, what are you doing down here?"

I close the inner house door behind me and walk over. "Where are you going at this hour?"

A flash of guilt shines in his eyes, but he recovers fast and narrows them. "None of your business, *sis*. Go back to bed."

"I'm not your sister, jackass," I hiss. "And I'm not going to bed unless you come with me."

His eyes widen, then a slow grin unfurls on his lips. "Is that an invitation?"

Fuck. I misspoke. "I didn't mean it like that."

He props his bike against the wall and shortens the distance between us. I try to escape, but he's faster and pushes me against the storage unit behind me, resting his hands on either side of my head, effectively caging me in.

"Don't lie to me, kitty cat. Why did you follow me out here?"

"I want to know where you're going at this hour. Are you meeting someone?"

He chuckles. "Don't tell me you're jealous."

"I'm not jealous," I snap.

He grabs my chin roughly. "You're such a little liar. Tell me the truth."

I don't answer right away, but his eyes never stray from mine. He's trying to read my mind. My heart is beating savagely inside my rib cage, anticipating an attack of the best kind. If Eric doesn't kiss me now, I might die. But I won't initiate it this time. I did that once. If he wants me, he needs to claim me.

"You'll have to pry the truth from me."

He laughs, and the sound is as wicked as his mouth. "Are you challenging me, kitty cat?"

"Yes."

Using one hand, he squeezes my cheeks and turns my head to the side so he can lick the column of my neck. As if that isn't torture enough, his free hand dips underneath my PJ pants until his fingers find my clit over my underwear.

"Ah, you're drenched for me already. You're such a good kitten."

"Fuck you, Eric." I push his hand off my face and glower, which isn't an easy task when he flicks his finger left and right over my clit, making me weak with need. I'm breathing hard already, making my glare moot.

"I'd rather fuck *you*." He grabs my hair, keeping my head in place, and kisses me hard.

I resist just to be a brat, but I'm dying to melt into his arms and surrender to him completely. He coaxes my lips open with his tongue, and I bite his lower lip. That makes him laugh. He pulls back, keeping his hold on a lock of my hair, and stares into my eyes.

"Do you want to play games, kitty cat?"

"No."

"Bullshit. I think you do." He inserts two fingers inside my pussy, making me gasp. "You like that, don't you?" He puts another finger in, turning me more feral.

I grab his jacket and pull him to me, needing his lips on mine, so he stops asking me questions I don't want to answer. There's no fucking *way* he's getting a confession out of me. He can never know how deep my feelings for him go.

His tongue is just as addictive as I remember, and his heady scent has already gone to my head. I want more than his fingers. I want him to defile me, rail me against the storage unit until I forget who we are.

"I need more, Eric," I whisper against his lips.

"Tell me, kitty cat. Spell it out for me."

I grab his face between my hands. "I want you to fuck me so hard that I'll have bruises for days."

He pulls back and shrugs off his jacket. I am about

to demand he takes his sweater and T-shirt off too, but he yanks my pants and underwear down and drops to his knees. "I want to make you come all over my tongue first."

He spreads my legs and dives into my folds, licking my clit with gusto. I take his beanie off so I can run my fingers through his hair. His bangs are long, perfect for pulling. Eric alternates between sucking and running circles around my sensitive nub, sending beats of desire through my body. Then he moves his mouth lower and rims my entrance with his tongue, making me jump a little.

"Easy, kitten," he murmurs then bites the inside of my thigh softly. It's enough to send another ripple of pleasure through me.

"You're killing me, Eric."

"Not yet," he chuckles, then plunges his tongue inside me.

I yank his hair harder, trying to keep my moans quiet. But he's merciless with his wicked tongue, and I'm unraveling quickly.

His fingers graze the side of my right leg, giving me goose bumps. "Put your leg over my shoulder, Val."

I do as he says, and like this, he can really go deeper with his tongue. But I soon find out he has ulterior motives. While he's eating me out, he teases my other hole with his finger.

"Ohh... that's good. Don't stop."

He inserts a finger in me, and the onslaught of different sensations pushes me over the edge faster than I can anticipate. I'm not prepared, and my response is far too loud, especially in the dead of night.

"Yes! Fuck me, yes."

I'm shaking from head to toe, riding the wave of pleasure and wishing it would go on forever. Eric doesn't slow down—if anything, he's even more savage with his ministrations.

"Anyone out there?" My father's voice cuts through the lust fog like the sharpest knife.

Eric pulls away from me faster than a ninja, and if it weren't for me leaning against the storage unit, I might have fallen over. I pull up my PJ pants a second before my father opens the door to the house. Eric is already by his bicycle with his puffer jacket in hand. His beanie is on the ground in front of me though.

"What are you kids doing out here?" Dad asks.

"I heard a noise and came to investigate," I reply. "It was just Eric."

Dad glances at Eric and frowns. "Where are you going at this hour, son?"

"I couldn't sleep, so I thought a bike ride would help."

My father's eyes bug out. "Have you looked outside? It's snowing like crazy. Come back in. I'll make my famous hot cocoa. That'll do the trick."

Eric's gaze locks with mine, panicked. Hanging out with my father is probably the last thing he wants to do after he was between my legs. But I don't want him to go out in the middle of the night anyway, so I say, "Hmm... I'd die for a hot cocoa. Come on, big brother. You'll love it."

He narrows his eyes. I'm not sure if he's giving me the death glare because I'm not letting him escape or because I called him brother. Either way, I win, so I simply smile in return, hoping he retaliates.

eight

VALERIE

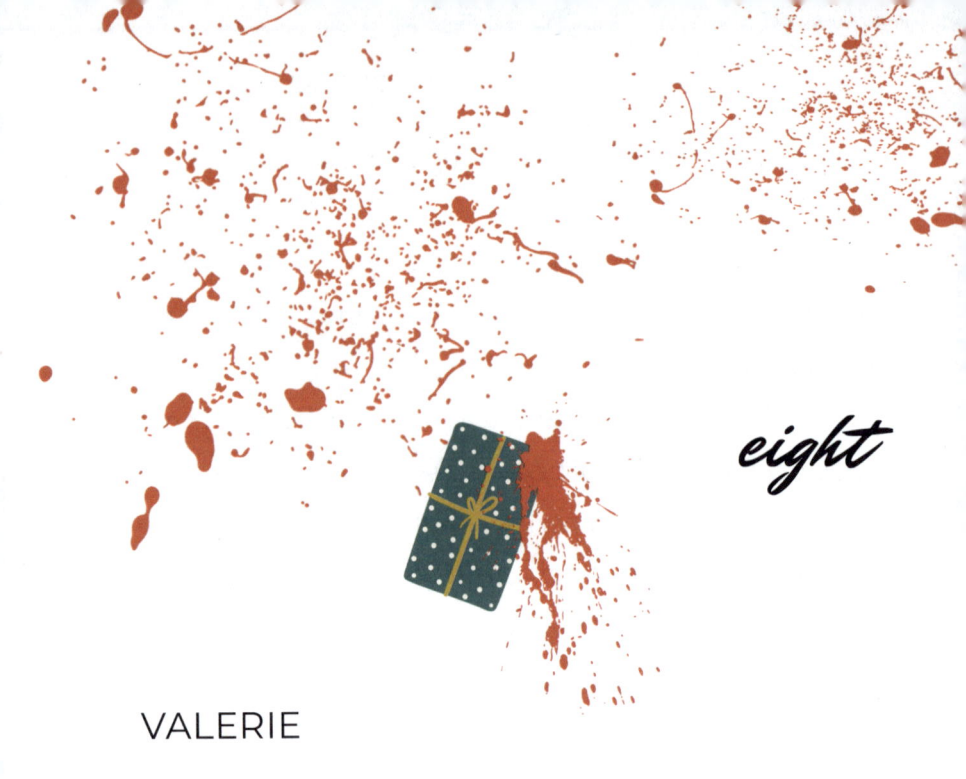

Eric didn't come to my room to finish what we started in the garage. I shouldn't be annoyed this morning, considering I had an orgasm and he didn't, but I am. Even the possibility that he might have blue balls doesn't make me less grumpy.

He's surlier than ever on the way to the church. I'm not happy either. Going to a mass in honor of Hansen is the last thing I want to do. The world is a better place without that asswipe. Everyone in attendance will be moping when they should be celebrating that the monster is no longer around to hurt people.

My angry feelings don't diminish my hatred toward Killer Santa though. He's another asshole in my book. He probably didn't even have a reason to kill Hansen and did it for sport.

Dad insisted we arrive together as a family, which means Eric and I are stuck together in a confined space. And yet, the gap between us in the back seat feels like a chasm, impossible to breach. He doesn't speak a word as he stares out the window. Maybe he *was* going to meet someone last night, and I ruined his plans. The thought makes me sad, not angry. God, he's turning me into a pathetic girl.

The ride is short, and once Dad parks, I'm the first out of the car. I take deep breaths of the cool air, letting it fill my lungs completely. Dad circles the front of the car and hooks his arm with Theresa's. She smiles at him, and he beams. They're so in love it's sickening.

"Try not to look so disgusted at other people's happiness, sis." Eric stops next to me.

I glance at him, but he's looking at his mom and my dad.

"I'm not disgusted." I start to walk, letting our folks take the lead. Eric falls in step with me but keeps a safe distance between us.

"If you cry during mass, I might puke," he says.

"Don't worry, there's no chance of that happening…. then again, I might do it just to make you nauseous."

He looks at me, and I see a hint of a smirk. "As long as you only do it because of me, then I'm okay with it."

My heart does a somersault followed by a backflip. One look from Eric is all it takes to make me go all mushy. I think if he touched me, I might combust on the spot. I don't know why I thought I could box up my feelings for him and forget about them. Eric is the type of guy who gets under your skin and leaves a permanent mark.

I'm still staring at him and not paying attention to where I'm going. I step on a patch of ice and slip, almost falling on my ass. Eric catches me, wrapping his hands around my arm.

"Careful, Val. You don't want to break a leg and end your track career."

"There's always archery."

His eyes widen. "Since when do you play with bows and arrows?"

I pull my arm free of his grasp. "Since I took a class and loved it. Turns out, I'm a natural."

We resume walking, and Eric asks, "How are you enjoying Hawthorne?"

My brows arch. "Are you seriously asking me about college?"

He shrugs. "Why not?"

"I like Hawthorne fine. They have a really good hockey team." I don't know why I added that last bit.

"I know. They wanted to recruit me last year."

That's news to me, and I don't know what to make of the way my heart clenches. "I didn't know that."

"It isn't like we talked much."

"Why did you decide to attend Clayton U instead?"

Eric doesn't answer, so I chance another peek at his face. His jaw is tense. Unfortunately, I don't have a chance to press him. We're about to enter the church.

The first person we see inside is Carol, Hansen's younger sister. I haven't seen her since Hansen's funeral. After his death, she went to live with her aunt out of state. She looks exactly like I remember, with her long blonde hair and big blue eyes. She always reminded me of a porcelain doll, pretty and perfect. But today, her eyes are dull and a little sunk in. She's lost weight too. I can't believe she's still reeling over her brother's death. Or maybe there's something else going on with her.

She smiles in our direction, and her gaze lingers on Eric. No surprise there. I've always suspected she had a crush on him. Maybe she was the one he was supposed to meet last night. I get crazy jealous again and can't help giving her a death glare.

After she greets our folks, she pulls me aside and whispers, "I didn't think you'd come, Val."

"Why would you think that?"

She takes a folded manila envelope from her jacket pocket and gives it to me. "Because of this."

Frowning, I open the envelope. There are pictures inside, and only when I get them halfway out of the envelope do I see what they are. My stomach twists savagely in my belly, making me sick. God, I might throw up after all.

I hastily shove those disgusting pictures back in the envelope. "Where did you find these?"

Her eyes are bright, full of unshed tears. "I'm sorry that Hansen did that to you, but he's not the real monster of the story." She glances over her shoulder, and I follow her line of sight. She's looking at her father.

"Did your father take these?" I whisper.

"I—I have to go." She hurries away before I can get in another word.

My body is shaking, and my throat is closing. I have to get out of here.

Before I can move, Eric steps closer. "What was that about?"

"Nothing." I pivot and walk out of the church.

The pest follows me. "Val, where are you going?"

"Leave me alone, Eric."

The crowd that is shuffling into the church turns to look at us. Great. An audience.

Eric grabs my arm, seeming not to care that we have witnesses. "I'm not going to let you leave until you tell me what's in that envelope Carol gave you."

Fuck. Of course he saw the entire exchange. I'm surprised he didn't get a peek at the disgusting pictures too. He's tall, and if he was close enough, he might have been able to see them.

"Let go!" I yank my arm free. "You're not the boss of me."

"I'm just trying to help."

"You wanna help? Tell my father I went home."

"How are you getting home?"

"Have you heard of Uber?" I take my phone out of my purse.

He narrows his eyes. "Are you really going home?"

I pause and hold his gaze. What does he mean? "Where else would I go?"

nine

ERIC

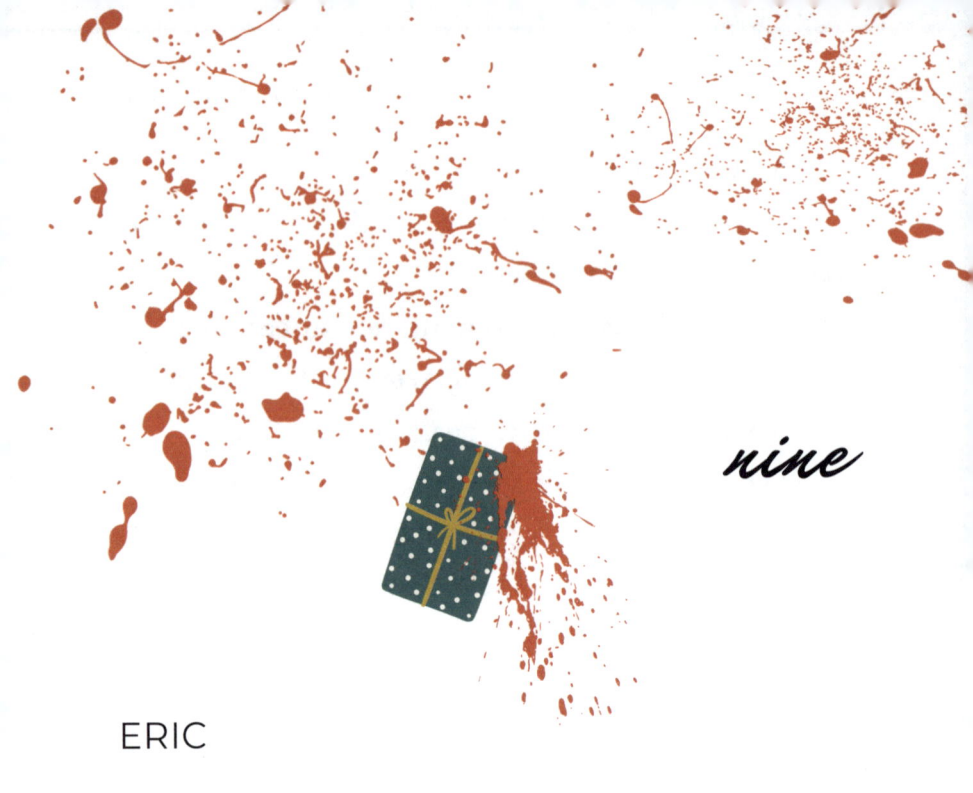

Valerie isn't home when we return from church, and that worries not only her dad and my mom but also me. I know whatever was in that envelope is the reason she didn't stay for the service. I search her room but find nothing. Either she hid it well, or she never came home to leave the envelope in her room in the first place.

I run downstairs, ready to go looking for her when she walks in the front door. At first, I'm relieved, but then annoyance wins. "Where have you been?"

She widens her eyes. "I went to the pharmacy. What's with you?"

I rub my face and look away. Fuck. I'm not acting like myself, but I never do when Valerie is involved. I usually know where I stand with people, but when I'm with her, I'm lost.

"Val, honey. We were worried." Her father joins us in the foyer, saving me from having to answer her question.

"I wasn't feeling well, so I went to the pharmacy to get Pepto-Bismol."

"Honey, why didn't you call me? I could have stopped and gotten it for you."

"It's okay, Dad." She shrugs.

I see the pharmacy bag in her hand, but I don't buy that she went only there. That's her cover. Where the hell did she go?

"Will you be able to work tonight?" Mom asks her.

"Work where?" I ask.

"I'm waitressing at the mayor's party," Valerie answers me then glances at my mother. "Yes, I'll be fine. Besides, I'm looking forward to it. It'll be a nice distraction."

Keith and Mom look at her with compassion, but her statement makes me sick. She doesn't need the distraction because Hansen is dead. She needs it because of what he did to her. I wish I could make her forget or at least carry the pain for her.

Mom turns her attention to me. "You should come, Eric."

I scoff. "Attend a stuffy party? Pass. I'd rather watch horror movies all night."

Mom grimaces, but it's Valerie who replies, "Halloween is over."

"Not to me, sis. Halloween is an all-year event in my world."

She rolls her eyes. "You're such a weirdo."

A weirdo who you like to fuck. The thought makes me smile.

I don't see Valerie for most of the day. I stay in my room, waiting for the opportunity to snoop in her bedroom again. My chance comes when she heads into the shower to get ready for the mayor's party. I'm beginning to appreciate the fact that Keith doesn't believe in locks. Valerie would for sure have locked her door.

I don't have to look long to find the damn envelope. It's still in the inside pocket of her coat. I have to bite the inside of my cheek until I taste blood to stop the scream that wants to rip from my throat. These are pictures of Valerie's rape. It happened in a cabin in the woods, and someone was standing outside, watching and documenting it for later. That's why I couldn't find Hansen and Valerie at the party. He took her to a secluded location.

I replay the scene of Valerie and Carol at the church. Valerie's face turned ashen when she saw the contents of the envelope, and then they both glanced in Carol's father's direction.

Son of a bitch.

My nostrils flare as I take deep breaths, trying to slow my accelerated pulse. Mark fucking Warner, the model citizen of Stanmore, was part of the whole thing. I put the pictures back where they belong and get out of Valerie's room before she catches me there.

I couldn't find a target last night, thanks to Valerie's delicious interruption. But now I don't need to search. Carol handed one to me on a silver platter—well, not me, but that's a technicality. I don't feel sorry that she's going to lose her asshole father one year after her brother met my blade. If she gave those pictures to Valerie and indicated that her father was the one who took them, it's because she wants Valerie to do something about it. Maybe she's also his victim.

To keep up appearances, I get comfortable in the living room and put on *Scream*, one of my favorite slasher movies. I want Mom and Keith to see me at home doing what I said I would. Valerie is the first one to come downstairs. I look over my shoulder and watch her put on a different coat than the one she wore for church.

"Leaving already?" I ask.

"I have to be at the mayor's house before the guests arrive."

I want to ask her to stay, but one, she'll say no, and two, I won't be able to sneak out later if she's around.

"Have fun."

She smiles, and it's chilling. "Oh, I will."

I narrow my eyes. Valerie is up to no good.

As long as she doesn't get in the way of *my* work, everything will be fine.

Halfway through the movie, Mom and Keith make their way downstairs. Mom asks again if I want to come to the party, and my answer remains the same. I finish watching the movie, and then I get going. I have to visit the bunker first. It's time for *Killer Santa Two—Sins of the Father.*

ten

ERIC

It takes an hour to retrieve my stuff from the bunker and get to the mayor's party. By the time I arrive, I'm a human popsicle. That's the drawback of riding a bike in the middle of the winter. But I don't have a car in Stanmore anymore, and I can't drive my mother's car and risk anyone seeing it zooming away from the crime scene.

The mayor lives in a huge red brick two-story house that's fully decorated with Christmas lights. But in a more tasteful and less extravagant way than most of the other houses in the neighborhood. This time, I leave my bike in a small park behind the house. The snow is high, so I drop the bike behind a bench, and after I get everything I need from my backpack, I cover the bike and backpack with snow.

I had to get rid of my coat and beanie, and now I'm wearing only my suit. There's no way I can sneak into a house full of people unless I look like I belong there. So I'm posing as a guest. I just have to make sure Mom, Keith, and Valerie don't see me. I circle to the back of the house, but before I venture in through the staff entrance, I pull out the flask of whiskey I borrowed from Keith and wash my mouth with it, swishing and then spitting out the whiskey a few seconds later.

Hell, this stuff is awful. It burns and has an aftertaste I don't care for. But it's needed for my disguise. I sprinkle a little bit of the whiskey on my clothes and neck for good measure. My character is a drunk guest who got lost, and I need to smell like I've been swimming in booze.

My body relaxes as soon as I leave the freezing temperature behind and step foot in the kitchen. Personnel are working furiously to get food and drinks out to the guests, and no one notices my presence for a moment. I keep walking as if I forgot how to put one foot in front of the other until I bump into a cook.

"Sorry," I say.

The man frowns. "You're not supposed to be here, sir."

I look around, pretending to be confused. "Shit. I think I took a wrong turn somewhere. I was looking for the bathroom."

The cook gives me directions, and I get out of the kitchen fast, but not before I purposely knock a tray of canapés down. "Oops. Sorry."

Okay, now if anyone recognizes me, they'll say I was too drunk to be able to shish kebob anyone. Out of the safety of the kitchen, I stick to the walls, keeping my face partially covered by my long bangs. This isn't the best of my plans. I prefer jumping someone when they're alone in the dark. But there's not a chance in hell I'll let Mark Warner remain unpunished. If I had known he was involved, he'd be long gone. He's already lived longer than he should, probably committing more atrocities because I didn't do my due diligence.

I've been here before and know the lay of the land. The mayor invited our family for dinner when Mom and I first moved to Stanmore. Keith is an important member of the community, and the mayor wants to play nice with the newcomers. I head toward the mayor's home office, on the opposite side of the house from the main party, which makes it the perfect location for a murder.

No one sees me making a beeline toward the correct hallway. I slip inside the office quickly, leaving the door partially open.

Then I put in motion my second part of the plan, which is to lure Mark Warner here. I take my burner phone out—it pays to be prepared for all scenarios—and send him a text that will make him want privacy. The dirty secret that put him on top of my list is the very thing that'll lead him to his demise.

VALERIE

I'm glad Eric didn't come to the mayor's party. He's a distraction I don't need. My entire focus needs to be on the task at hand. One slip, and I might end up killing the wrong person. After Hansen died, I kept working on the poison that was meant for him. I figured I might need it one day. Now, I'm going to use it on the person who probably turned Hansen into a monster—his father. This will be my first kill, and I need to get it right.

Mark Warner is one of the most influential citizens in Stanmore, owning half the stores downtown. He's also part of the city council. So he's at the mayor's party even though today marks the anniversary of his son's death. I won't have a better opportunity to end him.

It's an effort to serve the man during the pre-dinner portion of the event and not give him his special drink right then. But I don't want his death to be a spectacle. Plus, I can't be the one to serve the asshole his last drink. I'd become the prime suspect. I have to serve him the poisoned drink when he's alone.

I also want him to know I'm the one ending him. I can't gloat if there are witnesses around.

Most people who were at the church this morning are at the party. But there's a glaring difference. No one seems to be upset anymore about Hansen. They shouldn't be, but it just shows how fake these people are.

My chance for revenge comes after dinner. The band is kicking it, and the guests are dancing to popular nineties songs, including my father and Theresa. I'm glad they're having fun.

Mark Warner has his phone glued to his ear as he strides down the hallway. I bet he's going to the mayor's office. I grab a glass of whiskey from the bar and, without anyone seeing, squeeze a few drops of the poison into it. Then, I move close to the wall to become invisible and slowly make my way to the office as well. I don't know yet how I'm going to convince him to drink this without causing suspicion, but I'll improvise.

It takes longer than I care for to get to the mayor's office, and I'm shaking a little by the time I get there. The door is closed, and now I get the full blast of the pre-murder jitters. My pulse is racing, and my mouth is suddenly dry. If I miss this golden opportunity, I'll be furious.

You can do this, Valerie.

I bring the lowest point in my life to the forefront of my mind and let my rage wash over me. What Hansen did to me was despicable, but what his father did was worse. He documented the whole thing for God knows what reasons. Maybe he sold those images on the black market, or maybe he kept them for his private collection. Either way, he has to die tonight by my hand.

I hear a muffled thud inside, followed by a whimper. Shit. He better not be having a heart attack. I burst into the room and stop in my tracks. Killer Santa is hunched over Mark Warner's body on the floor, busy stabbing his stomach. What the hell!

"Not you again!" I blurt out.

He lifts his masked face, keeping his knife buried deep in Mark Warner's chest. We don't move for a couple beats. I do realize that I'm standing in front of a psychopath with no weapon besides a glass of poisoned whiskey, but I'm too fucking angry to care about that detail.

"You couldn't leave this one for me, could you, asshole?"

He yanks out his serrated knife and jumps to his feet. Ah shit. I do the only thing I can think of and throw the glass of whiskey at him. He leaps to the side, avoiding the hit. Fuck. Now what? I glance at the collector's bow and arrow the mayor has on display. I remember admiring it when I saw it for the first time. Killer Santa follows my line of sight. He knows my plan, so it's now or never. I run to the only weapon at my disposal, certain that Mark's killer will try to stop me. But when I turn around, he's by the open window, sneaking out.

"Oh no you don't."

I rush after him, but he's already on the run, heading to the park behind the mayor's house. Damn it. He's fast. I'm fast too, but his legs are longer than mine. I need to slow him down. I load the bow with the only arrow I have and take aim. If I miss, I can say goodbye to catching Killer Santa. Narrowing my eyes, I let the arrow fly. He lets out a yelp and falls down in the snow.

"Gotcha!"

I leap out of the window with the bow in hand. Killer Santa is lying on his side now and looking at the wound in his thigh. The arrow only grazed his skin, and it's now sticking out of the snow a little ahead of him.

He's still holding his knife, but when I come closer, he drops it and pulls his mask off. "What the hell, Valerie!"

Those intense blue eyes I know all too well are glowering at me. *Holy fucking shit.* Eric is Killer Santa.

eleven

ERIC

Valerie's eyes turn round as she holds my stare. I can't believe she shot me with an arrow. It's only a flesh wound, but I'm bleeding all over the snow and leaving DNA evidence behind.

"You have got to be kidding me," she blurts out.

"I could say the same thing. Why did you shoot me?"

"Because you killed Mark Warner before I could, dumbass."

Whoa. I wasn't expecting that answer. "You wanted to kill him? With what? Your killer wits?"

"It doesn't matter." She drops into a crouch next to me and inspects my wound. "Does it hurt?"

"No," I lie. "Thank God you have terrible aim."

She narrows her eyes. "I don't have terrible aim, jackass. If I wanted to kill you, I would have. I just wanted to slow you down."

"Well, mission accomplished. We need to go before someone sees us."

No sooner do I say that than I sense someone approaching. "Is everything okay?"

I turn and find a middle-aged lady staring at us with rapt attention. Fuck. That's exactly what we don't need. A nosy neighbor.

"Everything is fin—" I start, but the woman's eyes zero in on the Killer Santa mask next to me, and her eyes go wild.

"You're the killer!" She shuffles back. "Hel—"

Valerie jumps to her feet as fast as a ninja with my knife in hand and plunges it deep into the woman's throat, literally cutting her off.

My brows shoot to the heavens. "Jesus fuck!"

Valerie pulls my knife free before the woman collapses to the ground, her mouth open in a perpetual silent scream.

"What?" She looks at me.

"I can't believe you just killed her."

She stares at me as if I've grown a second head. "Why? Are you saying you're the only one allowed to kill people in this town?"

I get back on my feet, wincing when I put weight on my left leg. Flesh wound or not, it hurts like a mother. "I'm not saying that. It's just... I didn't think you had it in you."

"She was about to scream bloody murder, and she knew you're Killer Santa."

My heart beats faster. "Are you saying you killed someone in cold blood to protect me?"

She blinks fast, and when she swallows, it's audible. "You're my stepbrother."

Damn it, Val. Why did you have to ruin the moment and say that?

"We need to get out of here," she continues. "Where's your car?"

"I didn't drive."

Her eyes bug out. "You walked here?"

"No, I rode my bike."

She pinches the bridge of her nose. "For fuck's sake, Eric. You can't ride your bike now."

"I know, and whose fault is that?" I arch a brow.

"Fine. I'll pedal, and you sit pretty in the back. Where's the bike?"

"I hid it behind a park bench. It isn't far, but I can't really run now."

She steps closer. "I'll help you."

"Great." I extend my arm. "Can I have my knife back, please?"

She looks at the blood coating the blade and wrinkles her nose. "Here, take it."

"Why the face?"

"Your methods are so messy. That's why I prefer poison."

A warm feeling spreads through my chest. Valerie, my feral kitty cat, is as twisted as I am. "That's how you were going to kill Mark Warner, wasn't it?"

"Yes. Why did you target him?"

"We're not having this conversation next to a fresh corpse. Grab your bow and the arrow. We can't leave those behind."

"Ugh. Fine." Valerie picks them up in a huff and then returns to my side. "Lean on me."

I've already shoved the Santa mask and my knife in my jacket pocket, freeing my hands. I toss my arm around her shoulder, and slowly, we move away from Valerie's kill.

"Can't you move faster?" she grits out. "It's fucking cold."

"I'm going as fast as I can. You could give me a piggyback ride. That'll make you warm," I joke.

"You know what? It's not a bad idea." She slides my arm off her shoulder and squats in front of me.

"Are you sure you can carry me?"

She looks at me and smirks. "We shall see. If I drop you, it won't hurt... much."

I get on her back, certain we look quite ridiculous. But Valerie can not only deal with my weight but also move fast in the snow while carrying me; I sure as hell picked the right girl to fall in love with. Is there anything she can't do?

"My bike is over there." I point ahead.

"I see nothing."

"I covered it in snow."

"Of course you did." She sets me down, and I collapse on the bench, groaning. "You said you weren't hurting."

"I am now." I press a hand to my leg and find it drenched. "I need to wrap the wound, or I'll leave a trail of blood."

"I don't have anything on me to use as a bandage." She hugs herself, shaking.

"You're freezing. My coat is in my backpack."

"Let me guess, it's also buried under all that snow."

"That's right. Five points for Slytherin."

She narrows her eyes. "What makes you think I'm a Slytherin?"

I tilt my head. "Aren't you?"

She throws her hands in the air and sighs. "Fine. You got me."

"Do you wanna know what house I'm in?"

She starts to unearth my bike, working fast. "I already know."

My brows arch. "You do?"

She looks at me. "You're a Gryffindor."

My jaw drops. "How did you know that?"

"Please, you have Gryffindor written all over you." She drags my bike up and props it against the back of the bench. Then she opens my backpack, takes my coat and beanie from it, and tosses the latter to me. "I don't need the hat."

"Gee, thanks." I put it on and say, "Hand me the scarf too. I'll use it to wrap my leg."

She walks over instead of tossing it to me. "I'll do it."

I watch as she bends down and fusses over my leg. "Ugh, it's bleeding more than I thought."

"It's fine."

She looks up. "I'm sorry. If I'd known it was you..."

"Don't stress, but if you're feeling truly remorseful,

you could give me a BJ. I mean, your mouth is awfully close."

"You're such a pig, Eric." She ties the scarf tighter than needed, making me see stars.

"Fuck, woman. I was just teasing."

She gives the scarf a little bit of slack, and I can breathe again. "How is that?"

"Better. Now, let's go. It's only a matter of time before someone finds the bodies."

The shrill noise of sirens in the distance cuts through the silence in the park.

"Fuck. Too late." Valerie's eyes grow wider as she stares in the direction of the mayor's house. We're hidden from view, but we did leave footprints on the snow.

I get up and grab her chin, making her look at me. "They won't catch us. I promise."

Her gaze hardens. "You're right. They won't."

While she grabs the bike's handles, I shove her arrow into the backpack. The bow I'll have to carry in my hand. We can't leave it behind since it has Valerie's fingerprints all over it.

She can't ride the bike until we're out of the snow and on the street. We move as fast as we can. It's a little easier to walk now that my wound is bandaged. Once we reach the asphalt that's clear of snow, Valerie starts to pedal, and when she has momentum, I jump on the back of the seat sideways.

"Where should we go?" she asks.

"Home. No one saw you going in the mayor's office, right?"

"No, I was careful."

"Then there's no reason for them to suspect us."

"What about your blood on the snow?"

That might be an issue, but I don't want Valerie to worry about it.

"They can't know it was the blood of the killer. It could have been from another victim. Besides, I never left any DNA behind before. The police won't have anything in their system to compare to."

"I take it Hansen wasn't your first kill."

"No, he wasn't." She doesn't say anything for a couple beats, and my heart shrivels. Unable to help myself, I ask, "Does that bother you?"

"No. But it explains a lot."

"Oh yeah? What?"

"Why I was so drawn to you."

I stop breathing for a second. "Was? In the past?"

"Eric, do you really want to talk about our relationship now?"

"No time like the present. Go on, spill the beans, kitty cat."

She sighs. "You're a dog with a bone, aren't you?"

"When it comes to you? Yes."

"Why? Are you in love with me or something?"

Damn it. I wish I could see her face. Her tone is too casual, and I don't know if she couldn't care less if I was in love with her or if she's just trying to downplay her interest.

"What if I am?" She doesn't answer, but her spine visibly tenses. "Val?"

"I can't talk about this now, Eric."

It's not the answer I was hoping for, but it's also not a complete shutdown. I bite my tongue for the time being. As we put distance between us and the crime scenes, I begin to relax. But we're not out of the woods yet. We're still in the mayor's neighborhood, and pretty soon all these streets will be crawling with cops.

A minute goes by before I hear a car. I look behind us, and my chest tightens with worry. There's a black car tailing us with its lights off. *Shit.*

"How are your legs doing, Val?"

"They're fine. Why?"

"I don't want to alarm you, but we're being followed, and not by the cops."

"What the fuck, Eric. How am I supposed to not get alarmed? Who are they?"

"I don't know, but we should get off the street."

"Where am I supposed to go?"

The sound of a train approaching in the distance reaches us. There's a railroad that crosses through town not far from here.

"The tracks," we say in unison.

At the next intersection, Valerie turns right and takes off. The black car gives chase.

twelve

VALERIE

I pedal as fast as I can, but with the added weight, my legs burn. I hear the car rumbling behind us. It should have caught up with us by now. I'm not the Flash. But whoever is following us seems content to toy with us.

It doesn't matter. I have to lose them.

My biggest fear is sliding on a patch of ice. That would be a pretty nasty fall. The railroad tracks are only a few yards away, and the sound of the cargo train approaching is loud. The crossing gate arm is already coming down, and the lights flashing in warning. The only way for us to lose our tail is to cross before the train blocks our path.

"Val, what are you doing?" Eric asks me, panic lacing his voice.

"What do you think?"

"We're not gonna make it."

"We are. Trust me." My heart is racing, fueled by pure adrenaline, and when Eric wraps his arms around my waist, a jolt of electricity goes through my entire body, giving me an extra boost of stamina.

I slide through the small space, and the bright lights from the approaching train blind me. I push myself to the limit, my muscles complaining from the strain, but the effort is worth it.

Behind me, Eric holds me tighter and yells, "Fuuuuuck!"

We dash to the other side of the tracks, missing the train by a hair. A second slower and we would have been pâté. My heart continues to beat at breakneck speed, and my pulse is pounding so loud in my ears that it's drowning out any other noises.

I keep pedaling but slow down a bit, trying to save energy. My legs are shaking, and I don't know how much juice I have left in me. My harsh breaths come out in puffs of white air.

"Jesus fucking Christ!" Eric blurts out.

"I told you we'd make it." I smile, unable to keep my satisfaction bottled inside.

"I wasn't sure. I saw my life flash before my eyes."

Eric keeps his arm around me, and damn, it feels nice. It was worth being chased by God knows who, but I can't help giving him a hard time. He's making it too easy. "God, you're dramatic."

"I'm not dramatic. I almost pissed my pants."

I snort, then catch myself. "Ew. Spare me the nasty details."

"I said almost. Anyway, we need to find cover. Whoever is in that car will catch up with us once the train passes."

"I have an idea." I turn left and try to increase my speed again. Now that I know where I'm heading, I have extra motivation.

"Are you going to share?"

"I'm feeling nostalgic. I think we should pay our old high school a visit."

I see the school's big leaderboard sign ahead, all lit up and with a generic *Happy Holidays* message on it. In the distance, I can still hear the train. We'll reach the school before those fuckers are able to come after us.

"That's your plan? Breaking and entering?" Eric asks, not hiding his disapproving tone.

"Oh, so you can stab people to death, but you draw the line at that?"

"I'm not drawing a line," he grumbles.

I chuckle. Eric is acting like a big baby, and it's so at odds with his usual intense nature that I find it amusing.

"Why are you laughing?"

"No reason."

There's a pause, and then he says, "You should do it more often. I like the sound of it."

My cheeks become hot, and my galloping heart skips a beat before continuing to pump even faster, and not because of the physical exertion. Despite the dumpster fire this evening turned out to be, I'm giddy, like a stupid girl in love.

Valerie, you are *a stupid girl in love.*

I don't even know when it happened, and I've never allowed myself to hear the truth in my head until now. Maybe it was the glint of pure amusement in his eyes every time we argued or the patience he always had with his over-the-top mother. I knew he was miserable when he moved to Stanmore, but he never lashed out at anyone. All those little things kept adding up, and slowly, Eric gave life to my dead heart.

Only a woman in love would kill to protect her guy, that's for sure. I never pictured myself killing an innocent bystander, but I don't regret it. If it wasn't that woman's day to die, she wouldn't have been in that park. I'd kill many more to keep Eric safe, and that knowledge is freeing. If that makes me a monster, I'm okay with it.

"The gate's locked, but there's a hole in the wire fence toward the back," I tell him.

"I remember."

I stop the bike, and Eric hops off. "How's your leg?"

"It's stiff, but it's my ass that's the problem. I can't feel my butt cheeks." He rubs his fine tush, oblivious that I'm staring. Or so I thought. "I'll let you massage them once we're inside."

The butterflies in my stomach make their presence known. Annoying little bugs. I scoff, jumping off the bike. "How about *I* get a massage for carrying your weight for miles? My legs are jelly."

Eric hobbles closer, still favoring his right leg. "I'll give you a massage, kitty cat." He leans down and whispers in my ear. "On every inch of your body."

I swallow hard, trying to control how I react to his nearness. "Don't get any ideas. We aren't staying long. It'll be hella suspicious if we don't come home tonight."

"We can tell our parents the truth." He pulls back and looks into my eyes.

My brows shoot to the heavens, and my heart skips a beat. "You want to tell them we're killers?"

Smiling, he shakes his head. "No, Val. The *other* truth."

Oh, *that* truth. My chest tightens as I remember why we can't be together. I step back and start to push the bike toward the path next to the fence. Funny how I can kill for Eric, but I'm afraid to ruin my father's happiness to be with him. I'm a ball of contradictions. Maybe what I'm truly afraid of is to lose myself completely if I allow this strange feeling swirling in my chest to take over. None of the boyfriends I've had in the past made my world go off-kilter like Eric does. He's like a black sun, pulling me into his orbit. I've always thrived in logic and precision. Hence, why the making of poison is so satisfying to me. But when I'm with Eric, I become pure chaos.

He follows me, but I can't even look at him now. I'm already standing too close to a hurricane. One glance in Eric's direction and the flimsy hold I have on my self-control will snap. I'll be swallowed by the storm.

He doesn't say another word until we find the hole in the fence. "Does it look bigger to you?"

"Yeah. I can't believe they haven't fixed it yet."

"I can. They probably don't even know it's here. The

faculty seemed oblivious to everything that happened at school while I was here."

"That's true. They never noticed all the chemicals I stole from the lab."

"For poison-making purposes?" He quirks a brow.

"Yeah. My father didn't have all the stuff I needed in his home office. Hold the bike. I'll go through first, then you can push it through the hole."

"All right." Once we're both through, he asks, "Where to now? We can't simply bust in the front door."

"You can't guess?"

He looks at me, and I notice his nose and cheeks are red from the cold. That suit jacket is not doing much to keep him warm, but he hasn't complained at all. He never complains about anything, and that's another detail about his personality that gives me all the tingles and flutters.

His lips split into a grin. "The lab. You've done this before."

I return his smile. "I knew I liked you for a reason."

He arches a brow. "A reason? Just one?"

Heat spreads through my cheeks. I don't know why I get flustered every time this man flirts with me. I'd rather deal with Eric when he's a pain. I can handle verbal sparring with him, but when he's sweet, that's my undoing.

"Fine. Ignore me, kitty cat. I'll get the truth from you one way or another."

Ripples of desire run down my spine, making me shiver. I want him to use whatever weapon he has in his arsenal to get a confession from me. That's a dangerous wish to have when the man of my dreams is a killer with slashing tendencies. But I'm weak for Eric and his touches.

"I'm cycling to the lab's window," I say. "It'll be faster."

He covers my hands on the bike's handle with his. "No, I am. I'm done sitting in the back."

He's awfully close again, and I have to crane my neck to keep staring into his eyes. "What about your leg?"

"I'll deal with it." His gaze drops to my lips, and automatically, I part them. "If you don't want me to kiss you, kitty cat, I suggest you step back."

I want to scream *Kiss me, Eric*! But I don't. We're out in the open, and the people chasing us could see us from the street. I pull my hands from under his and increase the distance between us. Eric keeps staring at me with a shit-eating grin.

"You want to ride the bike, then go," I say.

"So bossy." He mounts the bike and takes off, going faster than he should before I have the chance to jump on the back seat sideways.

I manage it but keep my mouth shut. He did it on purpose, obviously expecting a reaction from me. Me not giving him one is probably driving him crazy, and I love it when he gets mad.

"There's the lab's window," I let him know when we're near it.

"How many times have you broken in over the years?" He stops the bike, and I jump off.

"Too many to keep track. I started coming here after hours freshman year." I try the window, hoping the latch I broke all those years ago remains unfixed.

"How many people have you poisoned since then?"

"A few obnoxious assholes that got in my way." The window begins to slide up, but it's catching on something and not moving up as easily as it should.

"And no one ever suspected foul play?"

I glance at Eric and find him studying me. My brows furrow. "I never *killed* anyone. Hansen Warner was supposed to be my first target."

His eyes grow larger. "Oh." He rubs the back of his neck, looking sheepish. "Shit, I'm sorry I ruined it for you."

My heart flutters. I don't know what side of Eric I

love more, the unhinged or the sweet one. I'm about to attack his mouth when he points at the window. "Do you need help with that?"

I step aside, making room for him. Without showing any sign of a struggle, he pushes the panel to the top with ease. *Show-off.* Then he moves aside and, grinning, says, "Ladies first."

"Right. You just want to check out my ass."

"Well... that's a bonus. Why? Would you rather I go first so you can check out mine?"

I narrow my eyes. "You're way too chipper for someone who got shot in the leg by an arrow."

"Only because *you* shot me." He winks. "Fine. I'll go first."

He props both hands on the windowsill and pushes himself up, then tosses one leg inside, then the next. I'm about to do the same when he sticks his hand out. If he had made a comment, I'd have batted his hand away, but since his gesture is wordless, I accept it.

The part of the lab that's far from the windows is pitch black, but I've memorized every inch of this place and don't need to see to know where to go. Eric closes the window panel and then turns to me. With him standing next to the window, his face is not completely encased in shadows, and I can see that his eyes are burning. My pulse skyrockets and my skin breaks into goose bumps, even though I'm far from cold in front of his searing gaze.

"How long do you think we should stay here?" I ask.

He walks over, invading my space. "Long enough for me to make you scream."

His mouth covers mine hungrily, and I open to him, welcoming his invasion. His hand is in my hair, twisting a strand around it. I stand on my tiptoes, tilting my head because I need him to kiss me harder and deeper. My skin is yearning for his touch, and my bones are already melting. I start to unbutton his shirt, but he grabs my wrist and yanks my head back, pulling my hair hard until it hurts.

"You're not allowed to touch me until you answer my question."

"What question?"

"What would you do if I were in love with you?"

My heart leaps to my throat and gets stuck there. I remember the conversation I had with Theresa, and all the reasons disaster will follow if I surrender to my feelings for Eric. But hell, I killed someone for him, and Eric killed the two monsters who hurt me. Our bond is stronger than any marriage. We're linked irrevocably. We have the same darkness inside us; we are a match made in hell.

"I'd kiss you until the end of time and never let you go again."

"Good, because I love you, kitty cat. You're mine." He takes my face between his hands and kisses me harder than before, his teeth nipping my lower lip.

I welcome the sharp pain, and it mixes with the elation spreading through my chest. Eric loves me. I never thought my black heart could feel so much joy. The need to be claimed by him in every possible way is overwhelming, and it overrides my sense of self-preservation. Who cares if there are people chasing us?

I curl my fingers into his shirt, pulling him closer, needing to meld myself to him. He picks me up, digging his fingers into my ass, and pushes me against the wall. I'm glad my waitress uniform is a skirt, not pants. Eric's hands are already underneath the fabric, tugging at my tights. He lets go of my lips and then places open kisses on my neck, making me wild with desire. I thread my fingers through his hair and pull it a little as I gasp for air. Then I hear the ripping noise of my tights tearing.

"Damn it, Eric. Now I'll freeze my tush off when we get out of here."

"It'll be worth it."

"If you tear my underwear too, you'll be fucking sorry."

"Shut up, woman." He grabs my neck and silences me with his tongue.

My panties remain in one piece, getting soaked through as he grinds his erection against my pussy. The friction feels so good that I'm already getting delirious. Then he squeezes my neck a little more and pulls back. "I wish I had a camera to capture how good you look right now."

"The picture would be all grainy without proper light."

He slides my panties to the side and inserts fingers in me—I'm not sure how many, maybe all of them, because he's stretching me in the best possible way. "You sure like to talk back, don't you, kitty cat?"

"Yes, and you love it."

He pumps in and out faster while pressing his thumb over my clit. "I love everything about you, and right now, I'm loving how your pussy is milking my fingers."

"I want your cock inside me, Eric."

He slows the pace of his hand. "I don't have any condoms on me, but I'm negative."

I'm sure there are condoms somewhere in this school, but I'm not going to suggest we go on a treasure hunt. "I'm on the pill, and I've been tested too. I'm all clear."

He goes utterly still, and I feel the sudden tension coming from him. "Who were you fucking in Seattle, Val?"

His reaction sends a shrill of excitement down my spine. I love a deranged and possessive Eric, but I won't let him know that. "Really? You're going to suffer from retroactive jealousy now?"

He pulls his fingers from my pussy, then I hear the zipper of his pants. He enters me with a hard thrust in the next second, scrambling all my coherent thoughts. "You're mine, Valerie. Don't forget that. *Never* forget that."

"I'm only yours if you're mine too."

He kisses my neck, sucking it so hard I know it'll leave a mark. Then he whispers in my ear. "You have my heart, kitty cat. Always have, and always will, even when it stops beating."

I let his words wrap around me like a fuzzy blanket. I feel the same way about him, but the words get lodged in my throat. I don't dare say them out loud yet.

"I'll keep it in a jar with formaldehyde when it does."

"You just know all the right things to say to me, beautiful."

He thrusts faster, and I feel like I'm going to end up

embedded in the wall. I kiss his neck, then bite it until I taste Eric's blood on my tongue.

"Fuck!"

"You like that, babe?"

"Yes, and I'll show you how much." Still inside me, he walks us to the teacher's desk, only pulling out to set me down.

"What—"

He yanks off my borrowed coat and turns me around, forcing me face down on the desk, pressing my cheek against the hard surface and keeping his hand on the back of my head. "Spread your legs wide, kitty cat."

"Eric…"

"Do it." He pushes the back of my shirt up, and then I feel something cold and sharp against my lower back, followed by a pinch.

My heart is thundering violently now, but I do as he says, and he enters me again. "That's a good girl."

This new angle feels even better than before, and the sweet agony escalates to new heights. Tendrils of desire curl around the base of my spine, making me soft and tingly all over.

Another pinch of pain makes me whimper, but it mixes with the pleasure building between my legs. "What are you doing?"

"I'm branding you, kitty cat, in more ways than one."

I try to twist my neck to see what he's doing, but he keeps my head down. Another sting follows, and now I know what he's up to. "Are you cutting me with the knife covered in someone else's blood?"

"No. I'd never defile you like that."

"Then what are you doing?"

"I'm carving my name into your back with my special blade, gorgeous."

"What the hell! You're such a psycho."

This is sick, and it's beautiful, and hell, I don't know why I was so afraid of the magnitude of my feelings for him. I let them consume me.

"Yes, and you love it." He pulls the knife away from my skin, but only to ram into me harder with his cock, making me move forward on the desk. "Say it, Val. Confess."

"I'm not confessing anything," I grit out, but it's a lie. I'm close to spilling all my secrets to him. That's how far he's sent me spiraling down the rabbit hole already.

"Saying no to me just drives me crazier, kitty cat." He cuts me again, but I barely feel the pain now. He keeps working on his art while fucking me. I can only imagine what kind of crazy-ass scar I'll end up with. But it's okay. I'll get my payback.

"There. Beautiful," he announces. He must have put the knife down on the desk because he's now holding my hips with both hands.

With his attention undivided, he brings his game to another level. I can't feel anything besides his cock fucking me and getting larger and harder with each thrust. I squeeze him with my walls, trying to do something to him besides lie on the desk at his mercy.

"You take me so well, kitty cat. I love how fucking tight your pussy is."

I'd have said something snarky, but the pressure building from the onslaught finally explodes, and all I can do is yell a string of curses as the orgasm obliterates me.

"That's it," he hisses. "Come for me. Scream louder."

"Yes! Don't stop. Fuck me harder."

The desk is moving now and making an awful, loud noise. Eric keeps punishing me, sending me careening again toward pure oblivion. A second orgasm hits me, and the room starts to spin. I close my eyes, surrendering to the feeling, scattering into a million pieces.

Eric's fingers dig into my skin and his body tenses. "Fuuuck!"

He moves faster, chasing his orgasm, and I love that I'm doing this to him. I don't even know anymore how I was able to shut him out of my life for so long. When we're together, I feel complete. His cock throbs inside me, filling me up until cum starts to drip down my legs. I love the mess and the sounds coming from him. I never want this moment to end. But good things don't last forever, and after a final jerky movement, Eric goes still. The racket stops, and all I can hear is the sound of our harsh breathing.

He leans forward, releasing my head from his grip. "Say you love me."

I narrow my eyes. "What if I don't say it?"

"Then I have to keep punishing you until you do."

A slow grin unfurls on my lips. "Then you'll never hear those words from me."

thirteen

ERIC

I don't need to hear Valerie say she loves me to know it's true. I can read it in her eyes. It's my ego that craves the words, although I love that she doesn't succumb to my demands. Mixing pain with pleasure is an addiction, and like me, she wants that.

Leaning back, I zip up my pants, but Valerie remains bent over the desk with her eyes closed.

"Did you fall asleep on me, kitty cat?"

"No. I'm not sure I can move, is all."

I chuckle, and she opens her eyes to glower at me. "Keep laughing. You have no idea what's coming for you."

"I can't wait." I walk closer to inspect my handiwork. The lines of my name are a little shaky, but it makes them more unique. "Not bad. We should wipe it off with antiseptic."

"Sure. I have some right here." She sticks her hand in her skirt pocket, then takes it out again, flipping me off.

"We're in a lab. They must have something in here." I offer her my hand, and I'm surprised when she takes it.

"Do you always carve your name in your hookups' backs?"

My brows furrow, but my lips twitch upward while a pleasant feeling spreads through my chest. "Who's suffering from retroactive jealousy now?"

"I'm not." She pouts, crossing her arms.

I grab her shoulders and invade her space, bringing my mouth inches from hers. "Why would I write my name on anyone else? You're the only woman for me, kitty cat, have been since I met you."

"Good."

I give her a quick peck on the lips. "You're cute when you're jealous."

"I'm not jealous," she insists, then steps away from me, grabs my switchblade from the table and puts it in her pocket. "Let's look for the antiseptic and then figure out what to do next."

I pull my phone from my jacket pocket. "Shit. My mother called five times already."

Valerie turns to me. The room isn't as dark anymore now that my eyes have adjusted to the gloom, and I can see her eyes go round. "They must have gotten home already."

"Where's your phone?"

"In my purse... which is still at the mayor's house."

Hell, that's not ideal, but I can't let Valerie notice that I'm concerned. "Let's take care of your new tat and worry about your purse later."

"We probably should clean your wound as well."

I forgot about that, too distracted fucking Valerie into oblivion. "Yeah, good idea."

"I think I know where the antiseptic could be. Call your mother before she sends the cops looking for us, thinking we're missing."

I've never been in such a messy situation before. We left way too much evidence behind. I've never feared getting caught because I've always planned my kills carefully. This is new territory for me, and it's making me edgy in an unpleasant way.

"I'll text her."

"What are you going to say?"

"That I went out to grab a bite to eat. As for you, you should tell them the truth."

"What?" Her voice rises.

"Tell them you walked in on Killer Santa murdering Mark Warner and that you chased after him, but he overwhelmed you and took you hostage."

"That's insane. They'll ask me questions for days."

"You're probably the only staff missing from the mayor's house. The police already know that. Trust me, the closer you stick to the truth, the more believable you'll sound."

She bites her lower lip, drawing my eyes to her mouth. As tight as my chest feels with worry that our story might not be airtight, my dick is already coming alive again, but we don't have time for a second round now.

I send a quick text to Mom, telling her I went for a bike ride and that I'm stopping at a fast-food joint to eat something. I'll have to do that so my story adds up, but first, I need to get rid of my bloodstained clothes and return my tools to the bunker. Valerie is already rummaging through a storage cabinet.

"I thought they kept that cabinet locked."

"They do, but I figured out the combination years ago, and Mr. Fisk is a creature of habit. He hasn't changed it." She turns around, holding a small bottle in her hand. "Got it."

My phone screen flashes with a message from Mom. I glance at it quickly, which is enough to see her freak-out message in all caps.

KILLER SANTA IS BACK.

"What is it?" Valerie comes closer.

"They've already attributed the murders to Killer Santa."

Her eyes bug out. "How? I killed the only witness."

"I'm sure it has more to do with the manner in which Mark Warner and that woman were killed. Don't worry, my identity is safe."

Or Mom's message would have been very different.

"Right." Valerie glances at the bottle in her hand, then looks up again. "Would you mind?"

I rub her cheek. "Sure, kitty cat."

"Be careful."

"Of course. I have a vested interest in my name healing well." I wink at her, which only makes her glare at me.

"I could use a clean piece of cloth or cotton ball to apply the antiseptic."

"There's nothing in the cabinet. Just pour it over my back." She returns to the desk and bends over, pressing her stomach flat against the surface. My gaze drops to her ass, and my erection is once again straining against my pants.

"Don't get any ideas," she says in a tone that's equal measures serious and wistful.

"Too late for that."

She looks over her shoulder. "I'm serious, Eric. I want to go home."

My stomach twists painfully as an unusual feeling—for me—pierces my chest. Guilt is not an emotion I get often. But it's my fault Valerie's in this situation. If I hadn't been so gung ho about killing Mark Warner tonight, she would have succeeded in ending the man in a cleaner way.

"Okay, kitty cat. I'll take you home after I clean your back. Brace yourself. This might sting a little."

"It won't hurt more than the actual carving."

I bite my tongue. This might actually be much worse. I got carried away, needing to mark Valerie with my name. For this, I don't feel remorse. I love that Valerie has my name imprinted on her skin forever. I pour the liquid over her back, and her entire body tenses.

"Motherfucker!" she yells.

"Sorry."

"That's what you call a little sting? Son of a bitch. Eric, if you weren't the love of my life, I'd kill you."

I freeze, but my heart takes off at the speed of light. "What did you say?"

"Shit," she mumbles, keeping her face away from view.

"I'm the love of your life?" I can't help the smile that blossoms on my lips.

Before Valerie can reply, I sense a disturbance in the air. The small hairs on the back of my neck stand on end. There's someone else in the room.

"Aw, isn't that sweet?" a female voice asks from the door.

Valerie jumps to her feet and stands next to me. "Who the fuck are you?"

As the owner of the voice moves closer to us and out of the darker side of the room, my jaw drops. "Carol?"

"Hello, Eric."

Before I can say or do anything, a horrible pain flares on the back of my head, then everything goes black.

fourteen

VALERIE

I watch in horror as Eric collapses to the ground, and I can't stop his fall, thanks to the beefy hands grabbing my arms. Carol didn't come alone.

"Let go of me!" I try to jerk free, and when that doesn't work, I stomp on their instep.

"Fuck!" the guy curses, releasing me.

"Amateur." A second guy zaps me with a Taser gun as I begin to spin around.

My entire body convulses, and pain, unlike anything I've ever felt, rushes through me. I lose control of my legs and fall to the floor next to Eric. Bobby's ugly mug comes into my line of vision while he keeps zapping me, and as the electric current renders my body useless, I stare at Eric, hoping to catch any sign he's still alive. The idea of him being gone makes me want to scream and destroy everything in my path, starting with Carol and her accomplices.

She moves closer, leaning forward. "You two made a mess of things, didn't you?"

My jaw is locked tight, and I can't ask all the questions bouncing around in my head. The only thing I'm certain of is that Carol set me up. I don't even know if Mark Warner took those awful pictures.

"You must be wondering what I'm doing here." She smiles in a chilling way. "You took something from me, and you got away with it. I had to make sure you'd pay for it this time."

Bobby steps back, and the relief of no longer being electroshocked is immediate.

"Took what from you?" I force the words out.

Her face twists into an ugly mask. "You took Hansen from me, you bitch!" She kicks me in the ribs, and white-hot pain almost makes me pass out.

"I didn't take him from you, but I wish I had. He was a piece-of-shit rapist." I expect another kick, but

Carol takes a deep breath instead and straightens her coat.

"You're not going to goad me into killing you quickly. I waited a year to get my revenge, and I'm going to savor it."

Fuck, now I wonder if her father sent her away because he knew there was something seriously wrong with her.

"Why did you set me up to kill your father?" I ask, trying to buy time and hopefully recover my ability to move. I've pocketed Eric's switchblade, but I must use it at the right time. I'll have only one shot.

"Because he found out about Hansen and me, and he wanted to have me committed."

Hell. Mark Warner was innocent, then. That would have been my next question, but then what Carol is saying finally sinks in.

"You and Hansen were *together*?"

"He was the love of my life!"

"Ew, barf," I blurt out. My reaction is totally legit and without any intention of making Carol lose control. She was fucking her own brother. It makes my relationship with Eric innocent in comparison.

"Go on, waste your breath judging me. It won't change your fate."

"What the hell do you want with me?"

She laughs like she's a villain in some Disney movie. "I'm going to let the boys have fun with you, and then I'm going to carve you up like a turkey."

Jesus, how come I never noticed how insane Carol is? I always knew Eric was different, but I had no clue about Carol. She totally flew under my psycho radar.

"What about Eric?"

"Hmm…" She drops into a crouch next to him and pushes his bangs off his forehead, driving me insane with jealousy. I want to yell *Don't touch him!* but it'd clue her in that I'm in love with him. She might have overheard us before revealing herself, but if she didn't, I can't let her have that leverage over me. *The first thing I'll do is chop your hands off, bitch.*

"I always had a soft spot for Eric. I guess he can take Hansen's place," she continues.

My stomach twists, and I nearly puke. But I'm also relieved. She doesn't know Eric was the one who killed Hansen, even though I told her I didn't kill that asshole. Fuck. Maybe she's too obsessed with Eric to realize he's the killer.

I look at the other goon next to Bobby and recognize Doug Michaels, who was also Hansen's and Eric's hockey teammate.

"I can't wait to make you pay for kicking me, bitch." Bobby grabs me by the hair and starts to pull me up, and I want him to think I haven't yet recovered control of my limbs. I need to catch him off guard when I slice his throat open. So, instead of punching him, I scream.

"Shut up, you fucking cunt!"

"No one can hear her." Doug laughs. "Let her scream."

Adrenaline is shooting through my veins, and my heart feels like it's going to leap out of my chest.

"Doug, help me with Eric," Carol pipes up.

"What are you going to do with him?"

"Well, I want to have some fun too." She stares at Eric with a demented look on her face.

"Hell, is he going to be part of our group now?" Bobby asks. "He's a fucking snob."

"Yeah, I don't feel like sharing you with one more dude," Doug chimes in.

Oh, dissent among assholes. I can work with that. "Are you guys dumb or something? She's always had a thing for Eric. She'll ditch you losers once she gets him."

"No, she won't, bitch." Bobby pulls my hair harder. "You don't know what you're talking about."

Carol laughs. "Don't even try to get Bobby and Doug to turn on me, bitch. They like my pussy too much."

Ah, hell, they're totally whipped then. "And you're okay with them fucking me?"

"I'm more than okay with it because you're going to hate every second of it." She looks at Doug and snaps her fingers. "What are you waiting for? We need to tie Eric up before he wakes up."

Doug hooks his arms under Eric's armpits and lifts him off the floor and onto a chair. Carol pulls out a few zip ties and uses one to fasten his wrists behind his back. Doug crouches in front of Eric, and oh, how I wish he'd wake up now and bash Doug's face in with a power kick. But he remains unconscious, and Doug proceeds to secure his ankles to the chair legs.

Bobby must have bought the ruse that I can't use my legs because he releases my hair and grabs my arms, then pulls me up and over his shoulder as if I weigh nothing. "Put me down, asshole."

He ignores me, which I'd known he would. I'm hoping the sound of my voice will bring Eric back, but no such luck. When Bobby moves away from the others, I tense, knowing the time to show my hand is approaching.

"Hey, where are you taking her?" Doug asks.

"I'm not fucking her in the lab. This room gives me the creeps." He veers for the door, and it takes a Herculean effort to keep pretending I'm useless. I hate that I'm leaving Eric alone with Carol when he can't defend himself.

"Wait for me, dumbass." Doug comes after us.

Before Bobby walks out of the lab room, I hear Carol say to Eric. "Alone at last."

Fury rushes through my veins, but instead of unleashing it now while I'm at a disadvantage, I bide my time. "Where are you taking me?"

"To my favorite place in this school."

"The cafeteria?"

He scoffs. "No. Why would that be my favorite place?"

Oh, he's chatty now. I suspected this idiot was putting on a show for Carol. He's not as psychopathic as he was trying to be. Too bad for him, I am.

"Because you like to eat."

Doug laughs. "She's not wrong."

"Shut up, asshole." He keeps walking for several minutes until we're on the other side of the school building. Then he stops suddenly and kicks something—a door, judging by the sound of splintering wood. "Turn on the lights," he orders as he strides into the dark room.

"You're not the boss of me," Doug retorts, but the light turns on just the same, and I see where we are. The workshop.

My pulse accelerates, but not because of fear. They couldn't have brought me to a better place with all these sharp tools at my disposal. But I'm conscious that time is running out. I need to end these motherfuckers fast so I can deal with Carol.

"Oh, this is *so* much better than the cafeteria," I say.

"Are you mocking me, bitch?" He sets me down on a bench and glowers at me.

I figure Bobby and Doug aren't the sharpest tools in the shed if they allow themselves to be manipulated by Carol. I bet I can make their loyalty waver now that she's not around. My plan is puke inducing, but desperate times, desperate measures.

I widen my eyes innocently. "Not at all. I've always had a thing for guys who know how to use power tools."

His brows arch and his stupid lips part, making him look more idiotic than normal. Okay, he's hooked—now I just have to reel him in.

Doug steps closer, holding his junk. "I got the power tools right here, babe."

Keeping the disgust off my face is hard, but I do my best. I lean on my forearms, pulling my skirt up and sticking my hand in the pocket with Eric's switchblade. With my tights in tatters, I'm giving Dumb and Dumber an unrestricted view of my black panties. "Can't wait to feel them between my legs."

Oh my God, I'm laying it on so thick, if these two idiots had any functioning brain cells, they'd see right through my bullshit. But judging by how their eyes bug out and their jaws slacken, I'm in the clear. "Now, who's first?"

Doug takes a step closer, but Bobby blocks his path. "Don't even think about it, bro. I carried the bitch here."

I try not to show how repulsed I am when Bobby pulls out his unimpressive dick and spreads my legs wider. He leans down, bringing his ugly face close to mine. I always thought his forehead was too wide and protruding, making him look like a Neanderthal. When he presses the tip of his dick against my entrance over my panties, my entire body goes tense. I can't see Doug anymore with the way Bobby is blocking my view, but it's now or never. I pull the switchblade out of my pocket and slice Bobby's throat.

His eyes grow larger, and he starts to gurgle blood. I shove him off before he collapses on top of me.

"What the hell!" Doug shouts.

I jump off the bench, but now that I don't have the element of surprise, I can't strike him easily. He jumps out of reach, and then runs toward the tool wall. He's going for the axe. Shit. I need something bigger than this small knife. I look around... and my eyes focus on the table saw.

"You're gonna pay for killing Bobby, cunt." Doug comes at me with the axe. I jump out of the way, avoiding the deadly blade by a hair.

Holy shit! That was close. My heart is beating too fast now, and I gasp for air. My entire body is shaking, but I don't dare turn my back to him and run. I'm fast, but I'm sure he's faster. Curse those fucking hockey players and their long legs. I'd rather face him so I can avoid his swings, and maybe I'll have a chance to use my small weapon. But walking backward proves to be a bad idea. I trip over something and lose my balance, my back hitting the hard edge of one of the benches.

Doug is gripping the axe with both hands as he raises it above his head. I freeze for a second as fear takes over. Then I think about Eric at Carol's mercy and snap out of it. By a miracle, I manage to avoid getting sliced in half, and he ends up embedding the axe in the table behind me. He can't dislodge it fast enough, and I don't waste those seconds. I plunge my switchblade into his side.

He lets out a roar and yanks the axe free from the table. I can't pull my knife free, and it remains stuck in him. Doug's dark eyes have gone completely rabid now, and I know my death is near. I shuffle back but hit my ass against another table. Fuck. I'm trapped. Blindly, I touch the surface behind me, hoping my hands can find a heavy object to throw at him. My fingers brush something sharp. I get cut, but I also know now that I'm standing in front of the table saw. Keeping my eyes on Doug, I lift the saw's protective guard just as Doug prepares to deliver the killing blow.

"You're dead, bitch." He swings the axe at a side angle, aiming for my neck. Instead of trying to jump or run, I flip the table saw on and drop into a crouch, punching his junk as his momentum propels him toward me.

He groans, staggering forward, and then falls on the table saw. The wet noise of muscle being sliced is the most satisfying thing I've ever heard. Still in a crouch, I shuffle to the side and then unfurl. Doug's eyes are wide and blank, and the pool of blood underneath him keeps getting bigger.

My breath is coming out in bursts, and my pulse is pounding loudly in my ears as I take in the room. It looks like a horror movie set. "Man, what a fucking mess."

I glance at the axe still in Doug's grip and consider using it on Carol. But hell, that looks heavy. I pull Eric's switchblade out of Doug's body and wipe off the blood on his shirt. I could sneak behind that bitch and slice her throat open, but then my eyes land on a thing of beauty sitting pretty on a table pushed against the back wall.

I pocket Eric's switchblade. I'm already covered in blood anyway. In for a penny, in for a pound. It's time to embrace my inner horror movie killer.

fifteen

ERIC

The sharp smell of ammonia jars me awake. I jerk in response and find myself tied up, my head fucking throbbing from the blow I received. The lights are still off, but I'm close enough to the windows that I can see my surroundings.

"Welcome back, babe," Carol purrs, standing in front of me holding a small bottle in her hand.

"What the fuck!" I try to break free of the bonds around my wrists and ankles, but it's futile. She must have used zip ties. I search for Valerie in the room and my pulse skyrockets when I find no sign of her or the person who knocked me unconscious. "Where's Valerie?"

"Who cares about that bitch? I'm here, Eric. That's all you should focus on." She runs one long nail across my cheek, making me wince.

"You don't know who you're playing with," I grit out, trying to figure out how I'm going to get free and kill this bitch in the next minute. With every second that passes, my heartbeat accelerates, and it's getting hard to breathe. I need to find Valerie.

"Oh, babe. You got it twisted around. *You* don't know who you're playing with."

"How did you find us?"

She scoffs. "Come on. There are only so many places you can hide and everyone who went to this school knows about the hole in the fence." She pockets the bottle and sits astride me, curling her arms around my neck. "If you do as I say, I'll untie you."

I grind my teeth, trying to keep my rage inside for a little longer until I can find out what Carol has in store for Valerie and me. "What do you want?"

She gyrates her hips, grinding her pussy against my lap. "I think you know. I've had a crush on you since you moved to Stanmore."

Nothing happens to my cock, not even a twitch. She

isn't Valerie. "Please don't tell me you went through all this trouble just to get railed by me."

She laughs. "Of course not, silly. The main goal was to get rid of my father permanently and make Valerie pay for killing Hansen. You're just a bonus."

Wait. She thinks Valerie *is Killer Santa?*

"Why would you want to kill your father? Did he hurt you?"

Her eyes soften. "Aren't you sweet to be worried about me? I guess you missed my story while you were passed out. But it doesn't matter. We don't need to waste time talking about boring things. My father is dead, and after I let Bobby and Doug do what they want to Valerie, I'll end her too."

So those two fuckers are involved in this? I knew they were morons; I had no idea they were psychotic morons. The worst kind. My heart is pumping like a factory now. I can't let them hurt Valerie while I sit here at this bitch's mercy. I curl my hands into fists and try to break free again.

"Am I sensing tension from you, Eric? I thought you hated Valerie."

"Release me," I grit out. I know it's the wrong thing to say, but it's impossible to keep a cool head and manipulate my way around this. I can't think straight, knowing Valerie is in danger.

"I think not. Make me scream your name in ecstasy and I'll consider it." She grabs my chin, digging her long nails into my skin, and slants her mouth over mine.

I bite her lower lip, drawing blood. "Ouch!" She pulls back and touches the smear of blood coating her mouth. "You hurt me."

"Come near me again, and I'll take a bigger chunk."

She slaps my cheek *hard*, making my ears ring. "You fucking asshole! And here I thought you could take Hansen's place."

My eyes widen as I finally begin to get the picture. "You were screwing your own brother?"

Carol jumps off me and starts to pace. "He was more than my brother—he was my soul mate. But then he got obsessed with Valerie. Got it into his head that he needed to find out if she was the cold bitch everyone in school thought she was. I hated it, but I understood his needs." She glances at me and even though it's semi-dark, I can see the crazy shining in her eyes. "Then she had the audacity to deny him, and when he took what was his, she killed him for it."

"You think Valerie is Killer Santa. That's why you showed her the pictures of her assault."

Carol stops pacing and stares at me. "I can't believe she showed you those."

"You set her up. Your father didn't take those pictures. *You* did."

Her spine goes taut. "Yes. Hansen asked me to. Then he died, and my father sent me away because he knew Hansen was more than a brother to me. He threatened to send me to an institution!" She runs a shaky hand through her hair. "I spent a year planning my revenge. I knew Valerie would return to Stanmore for Christmas. All I had to do was convince her that my father was involved in what happened last year, and she'd kill him too."

Carol's lips break into a demented smile. "And she did. It's just too bad that you got involved. I was going to let you live, but it's clear now you'll never be loyal to me."

Suddenly, Valerie appears in the open doorway. My breath catches. Even though I see only her silhouette, I know it's her.

Carol notices my attention shifting behind her and turns around. "You! Where are Bobby and Doug?"

"Oh, those two? They're resting now, after all the fun we had. But here, I got you a souvenir of our good times. Catch." She tosses something round to Carol, who catches it and then screams at the top of her lungs, dropping the souvenir—Bobby's severed head.

The sound of a chainsaw motor mixes with her

screams, and then blood splatters everywhere, getting on my face and clothes. Holy fuck!

Carol shrieks and shuffles back. "My hand, you cut off my hand!"

"That's for touching what's mine."

A goofy smile splits my face. That's my girl. I'm the one who belongs to Valerie. Happiness spreads through my chest like wildfire.

"You're fucking *crazy*!" Carol yells and cries at the same time. Man, what a scene. All I'm missing is the popcorn.

"You have *no* idea. Say hello to your brother for me." Valerie lifts the chainsaw, and there goes Carol's head, dropping to the floor. Her body follows.

My heart is beating so fast I feel like I'm having a heart attack. But it's pride that's swelling in my chest.

Valerie turns off the chainsaw and sets it down before coming to me. She grabs my face in her bloodied hands and looks into my eyes. "Eric, are you okay? Did she hurt you?"

"No. How about you? Did they—"

"No. I ended them before they had the chance."

"Kitty cat, please untie me because I need to touch you *right this fucking second* or I'll die."

Valerie pulls my switchblade from her pocket and cuts the plastic ties around my wrists and ankles. I don't give her the chance to unfurl from her crouch before I pull her up and kiss her harder than ever before. I need to consume her, devour her completely.

She drops the knife and circles my waist with her arms, bringing us closer.

"I was going out of my mind thinking that Bobby and Doug were hurting you," I murmur against her lips.

"I was worried sick about you too." She tilts her head back, and I don't miss the opportunity to run my tongue along the column of her beautiful neck before capturing her lips again.

My hands are already under her skirt, pulling her underwear down. "I need to be inside you, kitty cat."

She steps back, opening her button-down shirt. I follow and help her onto the desk, but this time, she's facing me.

"I didn't think I could love you more than I do now," I say.

"Because I killed Carol?"

"Not because you killed her, but because of *how* you killed her. It was the most beautiful thing I've ever seen in my life."

"It was damn messy but so satisfying. Now I get your killing methods." She reaches for my pants and pulls the zipper down.

"I hope Bobby and Doug had equally gruesome

deaths?" I nibble her lower lip and suck it into my mouth.

Her fingers curl around my shaft, and my balls tighten. I shiver, then release her lips so she can answer me.

"Yes, you'd be so proud." She guides my cock to her entrance, and then I take control, burying myself deep in her heat.

"I can't wait to see it." I run my tongue across her jaw and capture her lips again, then I ram into her as hard as I can. I already know this won't take long. There's too much adrenaline coursing through my veins and too much raw desire making me lose control.

Valerie throws her arms around my neck and links her ankles behind my ass while I pound into her tight pussy. "Eric, oh my God. This feels so good."

"I know it does, kitty cat. You're perfect for me."

She looks into my eyes. "I never thought I'd fall in love with anyone. But you snuck into my heart, Eric. I love you." She kisses the corner of my mouth. "I love you—" Then my chin. "I love y—fuck, I'm coming, I'm coming!"

"That's it, gorgeous. Unravel for me." She presses her forehead against mine, and we both look down. "Watch how beautiful your pussy is while milking my cock."

"I want to see you come all over me."

The orgasm hits me like a tsunami of epic proportions. I groan, pumping my hips faster. Midway through it, I pull out and cover Valerie's legs and stomach with my cum. She wraps her fingers around my cock and finishes working it until I'm all emptied out.

It takes me a moment to be able to breathe properly, and when I can, a burst of laughter goes up my throat. "And you said you'd never confess. Now you can't stop making love declarations."

"Life is too short, and I want you to know without a shred of doubt what you mean to me." She eases back and stares into my eyes. "You're it for me, Eric. I don't care what your mother says."

I frown. "What?"

Guilt shines in her eyes. "She knows about us. I don't know how she found out, but she told me to stay away from you. That's why I shut you down last year and moved to the opposite side of the country."

"I can't believe she did that." Hell, I don't know how to process this. I'm happy my mother found happiness with Keith, but knowing she's responsible for the most miserable year of my life is fucking disappointing.

"I can. She loves my dad, and she's afraid that he'll divorce her if he finds out about us."

"I don't want to hide our relationship from them. I love you more than anything in the world."

"I love you too, Eric." She kisses my lips softly. "But we don't have to figure that out now. There are more pressing matters." She looks at Carol, or what's left of her.

"I think Carol just helped us in that department." I smirk.

We lock gazes again. "You want to pin all Killer Santa's deaths on her, don't you?"

I nod. "Yes. If you think about it, all the deaths tonight *were* because of her."

Valerie's brows furrow. "I know. I can't believe I let her trick me into doing her dirty work for her."

"She fooled me too, and I was the one who got him first." I wait for the twinge of remorse to make an appearance, but I feel nothing, and I know why. In my head, killing Mark Warner was justified. I believed he had a role in hurting Valerie. The fact he wasn't, in fact, guilty bears no weight on my conscience. Carol was the one who killed him—I was just the tool.

"Do you want to see what I did to Bobby and Doug?"

I smile. "Do I? Of course. Let's go."

sixteen

VALERIE

It doesn't take long for us to set up the crime scene so the police believe Carol is Killer Santa. Eric cleans the Killer Santa mask with bleach to get rid of as much of his DNA as possible, puts her head inside his mask, then takes it off again, so if they find his DNA, it can be attributed to transfer. He also makes sure the murder weapon—his bowie knife—is clear of our fingerprints and covered in hers. The bow and arrow we turn into splinters of wood in the workshop and spread the small pieces throughout the school, keeping the arrow tip.

Our cover story is close to the truth, as Eric

suggested. I came upon Killer Santa stabbing Mark Warner and went after him. Eric happened to be cycling nearby and came to help. While Killer Santa was distracted killing the nosy neighbor, we rode away on his bike, but Carol followed us to the high school, and the rest is pretty much what truly happened.

"What about your shirt? It has Mark Warner's blood on it."

"I know. We need to burn it."

"Hmm, we could burn it in the school's kitchen, but what are you going to wear?"

He pulls a black shirt from his backpack. "I'm always prepared."

I can't help staring while Eric changes. He's on the leaner side, but his muscles are defined and begging to be explored by my fingers and tongue.

He catches me ogling him and smiles cheekily. "If I'd known you liked the sight of me shirtless, I'd have walked around the house without a shirt more often."

"Yeah, what a missed opportunity." I return his smile.

He walks over and pulls me into his arms, his expression growing serious. "I wish you'd told me about the convo with my mother when it happened."

"I didn't know you liked me that way. I thought you were just doing me a favor when I attacked you."

His brows shoot up, then he cups my cheek. "Val, how could you have believed that? I was crazy about you. I *am* crazy about you."

"But when did you start to feel that way about me? You barely looked at me when you moved to Stanmore."

His lips curl into a wicked grin. "I did look at you. So often, it made me sick of how you were turning me into a man living in hope and dying in despair."

My twisted heart beats faster. Only Eric can make me feel like I'm a sunshine-and-unicorns girl instead of the psycho I truly am. "I never noticed. I thought you hated me."

"No." He shakes his head. "But pushing your buttons and earning your ire were the highlights of my day. I did believe you couldn't stand me though."

"An act." I shrug. "I didn't hate you. I hated that I had such a crush on you from the start and you were oblivious."

His brows arch and his eyes twinkle with satisfaction. "From the start, huh? Was it my heartthrob face that made you melt?"

I slap his arm. "Man, you're conceited."

He laughs. "What? I have a mirror."

"Your looks didn't hurt, but that wasn't it. Do you remember when we were watching a documentary about the ugliest bugs and animals in the world?"

"Yeah. How could I forget? It was the first time we spent time together without our folks."

"You started talking over the narrator and coming up with the most ludicrous and bizarre backstories for those creatures. That's when I knew you weren't like anyone I've ever met."

Eric smiles. "So I have creepy creatures to thank for your affection." He leans down to kiss me, but then I tense, remembering something crucial.

"What is it?"

"The text you sent to your mother. The time frame doesn't line up with our story."

Eric seems unbothered by the plot hole. "That's an easy one to explain. Carol got my phone and sent the text to my mother to prevent her from calling the cops."

"Oh. I didn't think of that."

"I'm an expert at evading the police. That's why the cops in New York City could never tie me to any of my work."

She rises on tiptoe and kisses the corner of my lips. "You need to teach me all your tricks."

"I'd love nothing more... actually, that's a lie. There are other things that are higher up."

"Oh yeah? What?"

"Hmm, fucking your tight pussy, watching you kill like a vengeful goddess of death, which also leads to more fucking. So yeah, those two things are higher up."

His words and his proximity are already turning me on, and I can feel he's getting there too. Before Eric has me on my back again, I step away from him. "We need to take care of your shirt and then call the police."

He stares without saying a word, but I can guess he's considering not doing either of those things yet. His eyes are burning with predatory intensity, and my stomach flutters.

"Eric... don't get any ideas." I keep walking backward and closer to the door.

"Do you know what the best part of the hunt is, kitty cat?" His gaze darkens, turning dangerous. He's watching me now as if I'm prey, sending a thrill of excitement down my spine. Adrenaline spikes in my veins, making me giddy.

"The chase," I reply, then turn around and take off, knowing he'll come after me.

He laughs. "You know what'll happen when I catch you."

"Ha! You won't catch me."

"Wanna bet?" He's out in the hallway now, and I look over my shoulder. He's not running as fast as he can. He's taunting me. I turn around and jog backward instead of running.

"Sure. If you don't catch me, we tie up our loose ends and call the cops."

"And if I do?"

"You can do whatever you want with me."

The blue-tinted night-lights in the hallway give everything an eerie appearance. So when Eric smiles, he looks positively evil. "You're on."

"See ya in the cafeteria." I pivot and sprint away.

I know Eric is fast, and he has the longer-legs advantage. But I wasn't the star of the track team in high school for nothing. There's no chance in hell I'll lose this bet to him, even if a loss will feel like a win.

I turn a corner, and my shoes skid a little on the linoleum, making that annoying squeaky sound. Eric's footsteps are getting louder, which means he's getting closer. Hell, even with the gash on his leg, he's gaining on me. I can't let that happen.

I turn another corner, and this is the final stretch. I see the double doors to the cafeteria at the end of it. Not slowing down, I push one open and burst through. I'm about to yell victory when Eric's arms wrap around my body, and he lifts me off the floor.

"Gotcha!"

My heart is beating so fast and loud I can almost hear it. "Too late. I won."

He puts me down only to spin me around. "I don't

care." His mouth is on mine before I can offer a retort. I match his passion beat for beat, not caring that we have shit to do. Being possessed by him is my priority. When did I become so addicted to this man?

Sirens in the distance break through our haze of lust. Eric pulls back, his expression now serious as a sense of urgency drops on us.

"Shirt," we say in unison. We need to get rid of it.

seventeen

ERIC

It turned out someone saw a suspicious black car parked in front of the school and called the cops. That didn't leave us time to burn the shirt with Mark Warner's blood on it, so I just wore my clean shirt over it and hoped for the best. The gruesome scene the sheriff found kept him distracted enough that he didn't look at me twice. Besides, Valerie and I were clearly the victims who had survived a horrifying ordeal.

We gave our statements at the scene, and now we're back home.

No sooner do I step inside the house than Mom

turns me around and hugs me fiercely. "Eric, my boy, I was so worried about you."

I hug her back, but my gaze follows Valerie as she walks past us. "I'm okay, Mom."

Keith is not as affectionate as my mother is, so Valerie doesn't have to suffer from a bone-shattering hug like I do. Or so I thought. Mom steps back and pulls Valerie into the fold, hugging us both now. Valerie looks at me with a what-the-fuck glint in her eyes, and I have to fight the urge to laugh. But I can't control the little upward twitch on my lips.

"Let's go to my office. I need to check your injuries," Keith pipes up.

We refused to be checked at the scene by the paramedics, mainly because we didn't want anyone to see Valerie's new tattoo. Keith backed our request and said he'd examine us himself. Now, we need to avoid him too.

"I'm fine, Dad. It's Eric who got slashed on the leg. I just want to take a shower."

I narrow my eyes. *Way to throw me under the bus, Val.* But my injury doesn't have the implications that hers does.

"Are you sure?" Keith asks her.

"Yeah." She moves toward the stairs, and when her father isn't looking, she mouths at me, *Sorry.*

"All right, Eric. Let's check that leg."

I follow Keith to his office, which is a smaller version of the one at his practice downtown. There's an examining table, a white desk with a computer, and behind it, a cabinet with glass-paneled doors showcasing an array of drug samples and small glass bottles. With all these ingredients at her disposal, it's no wonder Valerie got so good at making poisons.

"Take your pants off and hop on the exam table for me, son."

I hate doctors. Have since I was a child. I always felt they knew there was something wrong with me, that they could tell I wasn't wired like most people. That was obviously all in my head. Those damn doctors were oblivious and cared only about prescribing medication I probably didn't need.

Being examined by my stepfather is a million times worse. I'm getting antsy. I glance at the penholder on his desk and get the urge to plunge one of his pens into his neck. But I stomp on that compulsion until it dies. It won't do to kill my mother's husband and Valerie's dad.

Keith has done nothing wrong. He's not on your list, Eric.

I repeat that mantra in my head until my accelerated pulse returns to normal and my brain is off the kill-now frequency. I sit, tense as hell, on the exam table and wait for Keith.

He puts on his wire-framed glasses and walks over. "Let's see what we have here. Lie down on the table for me."

Grinding my teeth, I do as he says and stare at the ceiling. When his cold fingers touch the area near my wound, I jerk a little and curl my hands into fists.

"Does it hurt?" he asks.

"No. Your hands are like ice."

"Ah, sorry about that. It is only a superficial laceration. We'll have to keep an eye on it for signs of infection, but it's looking good."

"Great," I try to sound chipper, but my tone comes out wrong.

"How did it happen?"

"To be fair, I don't know. It's all a blur."

I can't tell him Valerie shot me with an arrow. Even if someone finds the pieces we scattered all over the school building, no one will know what they are. The tip I kept it safe in my pocket. Val shooting me with an arrow doesn't fit the story we told the cops. Besides, that arrow tip has sentimental value now. It's a trophy of our triumphant night together.

"Maybe it's better if you don't remember. This is going to sting a little." He cleans the wound, but I barely feel the pain. "You don't need stitches, so I'll just put on a bandage to protect it."

"Shouldn't I shower first?"

"No, it's okay if you get it wet. You want to avoid getting soap in the cut though."

"Okay."

He finishes dressing the wound, and I expect him to tell me I can sit up. Instead, he says, "Thank you for protecting my daughter."

I turn my face toward him, unable to hide my surprise or the truth that comes out of my mouth. "I'd do anything for Valerie, even give my life to save hers."

Keith looks at me, and I realize he knows about Valerie and me. It's the anguished and conflicted glint in his eyes that clues me in.

"You care a lot about my daughter... more than a stepbrother usually would."

I sit up so I'm not in a vulnerable position anymore. "I love your daughter, and she loves me."

Keith clenches his jaw tight and doesn't speak for several beats. Whatever he says here will determine the course of my life. I can't speak for Valerie, but if she doesn't pick me over her father, it won't be a good day for humanity. I can already feel the darkness swirling in my chest. Getting bigger. Out of control.

"I'll be honest—it'll take me some time to get used

to the idea. But not because I don't think you're worthy of Valerie."

"It's the whole stepsiblings situation that's tripping you up."

He nods. "But after what you did for Valerie, I know you'll protect my little girl when I can't."

If he only knew his "little girl" is more than capable of protecting herself. But I bite my tongue.

"Are you saying you won't stand in our way?" I ask, needing him to spell it out for me because I'm still on edge.

"No, I won't. But I'm not ready to see you two together romantically. So while you're under my roof, no PDA."

I jump off the table and put my pants back on. I can't believe we had this conversation while I wasn't wearing any. "I can deal with that."

"Just... don't tell your mother yet, all right?"

Oh, jeez. What a great marriage those two have. It's almost laughable that they're both trying to keep my relationship with Valerie a secret from each other. But I won't betray my mother and tell Keith she already knows.

"I won't." I head for the door, but before I walk out, I look over my shoulder and ask, "When did you find out?"

He turns away, avoiding my gaze. "Last night, when I caught you two in the garage."

Fuck. I wonder if he heard us. He must have, but I'm not going to ask. I leave his office without saying another word and make a beeline for the bathroom, hoping Valerie is still in the shower. Keith said he didn't want to see any displays of affection, but he never told me I couldn't rail his daughter in his house.

eighteen

VALERIE

The water seems to keep running red no matter how long I stay in the shower. I didn't lie to Eric. It was satisfying to kill those fuckers in a messy way, but hell, the aftermath is killer. I think I'll stick to poison.

The bathroom door opens, and I turn around. "What are you doing in here? Our folks are home."

Eric takes off his shirt and then replies, "You're taking too long, and all this dried blood is making my skin itch."

"You're joining me?" My tone rises in pitch, but it's from excitement, not apprehension.

He removes his pants and underwear and opens the shower stall door. "Yes, kitty cat. I am."

"There's not enough room," I complain, only to be a brat.

He grabs my neck and pushes me against the tiled wall, so now he's under the hot jets. My heart is going a hundred miles per hour, but I don't fight him. Just watch, mesmerized, as he throws his head back and lets the water rain on his face. That arched neck is an invitation. I want to lick it, bite it, and I would have if Eric wasn't holding me in place.

He looks down, locking eyes with me, making my breath catch. His stare does something to my insides. I'm going soft in places I shouldn't, like my heart. My body is starting to melt under his scorching gaze. He keeps his hand firmly around my neck and reaches for the soap with the other.

"Would you help me, kitty cat?"

Holding his stare, I take the soap from him and rub the bar over his wide chest, following the movement with my left hand to lather him properly. I keep going lower, loving the hard ridges of his abs under my fingertips. Eric's breathing becomes shallow, and his eyes soften, but the desire is there, burning brighter than ever.

When I reach the tip of his rock-hard erection, he

hisses, making me smile. I drop the soap on purpose. "Oops."

"Careful now, kitty cat."

"Are you going to let me grab it?"

His lips curl into a devious smile. "Sure."

I drop into a crouch, and we both know I have no intention of finding the soap. Keeping my eyes locked with his, I curl my fingers around the base of his cock and run my tongue up his length. Immediately, he reaches for my hair, twisting his fist around a lock of it.

"You drive me wild, kitty cat."

"You ain't seen nothing yet." I run circles around the sensitive skin on top, tasting the saltiness of his precum on my tongue.

Eric hisses, then tightens his hold on my hair. Finally, I suck his cock into my mouth until it reaches the back of my throat. Eric seems to grow larger and starts to move his hips forward. I pull back, but not all the way, while using my hand to increase the friction over his length.

"Damn, that feels good. Do it again."

I repeat the same move a few more times before he removes my hand. I release his cock with a wet pop and ask, "What?"

"I want to fuck your mouth as if I were fucking your pussy." He parts my lips using his fingers, forcing my mouth wide open before replacing his fingers with his cock. "Be a good girl. Take it all."

He backs his words with actions, thrusting hard and ramming his cock into my throat. My eyes start to water, and I'm not sure if it's from the pain of his hold on my hair or the roughness of his movements. It doesn't matter. The shower stall is becoming an inferno, and I'm turning into flames. I reach for his ass, digging my fingers hard into his skin. I want to draw blood, knowing the pain will send him careening into oblivion. The veins on his neck are bulging, and the way his jaw is tense and loose at the same time sends ripples of desire all over my body.

He groans, "Fuck, kitty cat. You suck me so good. Dammit!"

Suddenly, he pulls out and brings me back up, only to push me against the wall and slant his mouth over mine while parting my legs with his. "I need to finish inside you, gorgeous."

"Then do it already."

He narrows his eyes, showing that hint of danger that turns me feral. His mouth claims mine again as he lifts me off the floor. My legs wrap around his hips, then he's inside me, destroying my pussy with his precise and hard thrusts. We're soapy and slippery, and yet Eric doesn't have a problem maintaining his hold on me.

My orgasm hits fast. I was already too worked up. Eric doesn't climax right away, even though I know he's close. He keeps ramming into me, stretching me in the best way until I fall apart again. Only then does he shout my name, his body trembling.

After a moment, he stops moving and hides his face in the crook of my neck. "I love you, kitty cat."

"I love you too."

I unhook my ankles and bring my legs down while Eric takes a step back and glances at his body. "I guess I'm still dirty."

"You're not going to get rid of that filth while I'm here."

"You're right about that." I make a motion to leave, but he leans his forearms against the wall, trapping me in. "I didn't say that you should go."

"Eric..."

He presses his forefinger against my lips. "Shhh... it's my turn to help you out."

I don't know where he's going with that until he drops to his knees and puts one of my legs over his shoulder. "You're still dirty, kitty cat, especially here." He touches my clit with the tip of his fingers before bringing his mouth to it. "So, so dirty."

His tongue darts out, making me gasp. I flatten my back against the wall, hoping I don't turn into a puddle.

The water keeps running, and in the back of my mind, I know it's a waste, but on the other hand, he's right... I'm still very, very dirty.

🔪🔪🔪

After our shower together, Eric and I go to our respective rooms to get dressed. I'm still tingling all over from the multiple orgasms, but exhaustion is finally creeping in. It's almost five in the morning, and my bed is calling me.

I'm wrapped in my bathrobe and drying my hair with a towel when Eric comes into my room via the bathroom, wearing only his PJ pants and no shirt. Hell, what is he trying to do to me? I'm quickly forgetting that I'm bone tired.

I arch one eyebrow. "Aren't you cold?"

"No. Besides, if I do get cold, you'll keep me warm." He uncovers part of the bed and slides under the sheet.

"What are you doing?"

Folding his arms behind his head, he smiles. "What does it look like? I'm sleeping here."

"Are you crazy?" His smile broadens and I know exactly what's on his mind, so I add, "Never mind. What about our folks?"

He taps the mattress next to him. "Come here and

I'll explain." I walk over, but before I join him, he says, "Wait. Bathrobe off."

"Fine." I let it drop and don't move for a couple beats, letting Eric take in his fill of me. His eyes miss nothing, and the growing desire I see in them sets fire to my veins. I turn around, showing him my new tat. "Had enough?"

"Of you? Never." He reaches for my hand and tugs. "Come here."

I finally join him under the sheet, but instead of making out, Eric pulls me flush against him and wraps an arm around my shoulder. With my head lying on his chest, I can hear the steady sound of his heart beating. It brings me so much comfort that it almost makes me cry. Oh god. What's happening to me? I didn't even cry at my mother's funeral when I was six. That was when I realized how different I was from all the other kids. Now my psychopath boyfriend is making me all mushy.

"Why are you unconcerned about being caught?" I ask.

"Your father also knows about us."

I tense and lift my head to look at him. "Oh my God. He told you?"

"Yeah, he fessed up when he was dressing my wound."

My heart is now pounding in my chest. It's insane

that I'm worried about my father's reaction when it comes to Eric, but I've done far worse things than loving my stepbrother.

"And he's fine with it?"

"He's getting used to the idea, but my heroic act tonight put me in his good graces."

I snort. "That's pretty funny when *I* was the one who saved your ass."

"He knows you're a badass, too, kitty cat. You don't need to be jealous."

"I appreciate the white lie, but I know my father thinks I'm a porcelain doll. It's okay. I'd rather fly under his radar."

Eric kisses my forehead. "Anyway, he doesn't want to *see* us together, but he never said I couldn't do bad things to you behind closed doors."

"What about your mom?"

He chuckles. "Get this shit. He asked me to keep it a secret from her."

"So we're just going to let them carry the guilt when it's no longer a secret?"

"Yeah."

"That's evil." I grin. "I love it."

"I knew you'd get a kick out of it."

I rest my cheek against his chest again and run lazy

circles over his stomach with my nails. "What are we going to do once Christmas break is over?"

"What do you mean?"

"We live on opposite sides of the country. It's going to be a nightmare to be that far away from you."

"Oh, I forgot to tell you. I'm transferring to Hawthorne U next semester."

I lift my head again. "*What*? How's that possible?"

"I told you they tried to recruit me, right?"

"Yeah, but you went to Clayton U instead."

"Well, that's not the whole story." He smiles like the cat who ate the canary. "I deferred my acceptance to Hawthorne to Spring semester, and they agreed to wait. The coach at Clayton U knew I'd be there for one semester, and he didn't care. I was only there to replace one of their star players who got injured."

"Are you saying you always knew you'd be coming to Hawthorne U and didn't tell me?"

"I wanted it to be a surprise."

My brows furrow. "What if I didn't want anything to do with you?"

He narrows his eyes. "I'd make you want me, kitty cat. We were always meant to be together."

"Make me, huh?"

Fast as a cobra, he rolls over me, nudging my legs open. "Yes, kitty cat, using any means necessary." He kisses me at the same time that he enters me, sliding in with ease.

Is it crazy that I love the fact he was prepared to do *anything* to be with me? Most people would say so. But I'm not like anyone else, and neither is Eric. That's why he's my person, my forever.

nineteen

VALERIE – *ONE MONTH LATER*

Tonight is the first time I've attended a hockey game since I started at Hawthorne U. After what Hansen did to me, I developed an aversion to the sport. But now that I'm with Eric—who is a fucking god on the ice, and I had no idea—I couldn't blame an entire sport for the actions of one asshole. Besides, Hansen's rotting in hell now with his two friends and his psycho sister. On the few occasions I think about them, I smile, remembering their gruesome deaths. Carol's was my favorite.

The Hellions are winning four to three against the

Jackals—Eric's former team—and I can tell some of the players aren't happy to be losing. The game has gotten super intense in the last five minutes, with harder checks against the boards and a couple altercations. One of the players from Clayton U tries to punch Eric in the face but misses. Eric glowers at him, and only I know that his death glare could actually mean death.

I memorize the player's name and jersey number—Kodiak, number twenty-eight. Eric won't kill him—he really tries to stick to his rules. Unless he finds out the guy is doing something amoral, then he'll put him on the list. I don't have the same reservations, but out of respect for Eric and to avoid drawing attention to ourselves, I adhere to his strict moral code too. But that doesn't mean I can't do something nasty to player twenty-eight. Diarrhea on his trip back to New York would be a doozy.

Eric is a right-winger, meaning he's always gunning for the goal. He's so damn fast he zooms across the ice like a comet. He hasn't scored yet, but he's assisted in the last two goals. He's thirsty for it though. His competitive nature is almost as intense as mine.

His chance comes during a power play for the other team. He intercepts the puck and takes off toward Clayton U's defensive zone. The goalie tenses, preparing for the shot. Eric pulls his stick all the way back, as if he's going to send a slap shot toward the goal, only to slow down at the last second, carrying the puck at the end of his stick and shooting from the other side. The puck hits the back of the net, leaving the goalie stupefied.

That's my man.

The horn blows loudly in the arena, and the crowd goes wild. I remain sitting and take a pull of my soda through the straw, hiding my smirk.

The intensity of the noise doesn't die down. It's the last minute of the game, and now Clayton U has an empty net. It's pointless. No matter how aggressively they play or how vicious their checks turn, they can't score. Patrick Walsh, our goalie, is a mean son of a bitch, and he guards his domain with ruthless focus. When one of the Clayton U players keeps poking at him after he gloved the puck, he goes wild and punches the asshole, knocking him down.

The referee finally blows the whistle, but he can't avoid the chaos that follows. All I see are punches and shoves. I lose sight of Eric in the melee, but I'm not worried. He's right at home. The more violent the game gets, the more he thrives.

The fight finally ends and the teams go their separate ways. The loser Jackals quickly head to the dressing room with their tails between their legs, whereas the Hellions line up to thank their goalie.

Eric bumps his helmet with Patrick's and taps his shoulder in an affectionate way. I always pegged Eric as an antisocial grump like me, but he's hit it off with his new teammates. I suspect some of them might share similar interests to ours, but it's too soon to tell. It's not like serial killers have social clubs where we share tips on the best ways to kill and dispose of bodies without getting caught.

Before Eric leaves the ice, he removes his helmet and glances at the crowd, looking for me. I don't get up from my seat or wave like a maniac, but he finds me just the same and smiles. Blood is dripping from a cut over his left eyebrow, and the sight makes me all hot and bothered. Eric, covered in blood, is one of my favorite things, and I can't wait for tonight's surprise.

ERIC

Valerie and I have been living together since I transferred to Hawthorne U. I had no desire to share a dorm room with a stranger, and she was on the verge of killing her roommate for real.

She doesn't wait for me at the arena like most girlfriends do. Being affectionate in public is not her MO, and very few people know that we're a couple. That makes for some interesting situations, and my favorite is when a random chick flirts with me in front of Valerie. I love seeing the murderous glint that shines in her eyes when that happens. It also makes me damn proud that she reins in her killer instinct for me and doesn't go on a murder spree. It doesn't take much for people to end up on her blacklist.

"Honey, I'm home," I announce as I walk into our two-bedroom apartment. The decor is all light and warm colors, and it's surprisingly cozy. You wouldn't suspect two serial killers are living here. It's also much nicer than any student housing I've seen.

My father is an asshole who thinks fatherly affection means throwing money at me. I never cared about money, but I'm also not one to turn it down. It means I can offer my black-cat girl things I wouldn't otherwise, not that she cares about that either.

Valerie walks out of our bedroom and comes straight to me. I drop my duffel bag and pull her into my arms, kissing her deeply. I'll never get tired of how she tastes or the noises she makes when I'm turning her on.

I pull back and look into her warm brown eyes. "Hi."

"Hi." She smiles back. "Great game."

"Yeah."

She switches her attention to the cut above my eyebrow. "How many stitches?"

"Just five."

"You looked hot with all that blood covering your face."

I run my thumb over her full lips. "You like when I bleed, don't you, kitty cat?"

"You know I do." She steps away from my embrace and turns to the two glasses on the counter. "Here, I made celebratory drinks."

I grab the glass she offers me and take a whiff. She knows I don't drink alcohol, so I'm curious about the red beverage. "What is it?"

"It's nonalcoholic Dragon's Blood Punch. It's a combination of Hawaiian Punch, apple and cranberry juices, and ginger ale."

"It smells good." I take a sip, enjoying the sweetness of the Hawaiian Punch mixed with the fizz from the ginger ale, but after a couple sips, I notice a bitter aftertaste.

Valerie is watching me with rapt attention, and her eyes shine with mischief. "What else is in this drink?"

"Just a secret ingredient to add some bang."

My vision turns blurry, and I begin to lose sensation in my body. "Val, what the h—" The entire room seems to tilt, or maybe I'm the one falling. Then nothing.

I open my eyes, and it takes a moment for them to adjust to the gloom. It's not completely dark. There's some light coming from behind me. I'm in the bedroom, that much I can tell. My brain is foggy though, as if it were stuffed with cotton candy.

I'm lying on my stomach, and when I try to move, I discover that my wrists are bound above my head. I look up and see I've been cuffed to the headboard.

"Val!"

"Oh, you're finally awake." I turn my head toward her voice, and she moves into my line of vision, wearing absolutely nothing.

My dick stands at attention in an instant, and it's not only her hot body that's doing it for me. It's also the switchblade she has in her hand that's giving me a hard-on.

"Whatchu doing?" I try to sound nonchalant as I stare at the knife, but my pulse is thrumming.

"I think it's about time you get your own tattoo to match mine."

"Kitty cat... please don't play with my emotions. I've been waiting for this moment for weeks."

"I know. I was waiting for the right time."

I notice then she's keeping her left hand hidden behind her back. "What else are you holding?"

She brings her arm forward, revealing a pink dildo. "Oh this? It's just another tool. Can you guess where it's going?"

"Your pussy?"

Her lips curl into a wicked grin. "At first..."

"Kitty cat... you're not implying...."

"I want to reciprocate what you did for me, babe. It's only fair I carve my name into your back while fucking you at the same time."

My heart is now beating violently inside my chest, torn between arousal and anxiety. This ought to be hot as hell. "Will it hurt?"

"Probably." She turns the dildo on and lifts her left leg, propping her foot on the nightstand and giving me a full view of her smooth, pink pussy, which is already glistening with her arousal. She presses the head of the dildo against her clit first and moans.

I squirm, trying to find a better angle to watch the show. "Kitty cat... come on. That's not fair."

"I know." She slides the device down to her entrance and slowly pushes it in. "God, this feels good."

Darkness swirls in my chest, and in vain, I try to free myself from the cuffs. I'm fucking jealous of a sex toy. "You're playing a dangerous game, gorgeous."

Her eyes are hooded already, burning with desire. "I know. Don't be angry, though. This is all for your benefit."

She removes the vibrator from her pussy and joins me on the bed, kneeling behind me and coaxing my legs open. "Let's see that tight hole, babe."

I stop trying to see what she's doing and close my eyes, groaning when she teases my hole with her toy. It's coated in her juices, and now I get why she said it was all for my benefit. But Valerie isn't keen on taking things slow. Without warning, she pushes the damn thing into me, making my entire body tense.

Fuck. It burns, but it's a good burn.

"How does it feel, babe?" she asks sweetly.

I open my eyes and turn my face toward her. "Are you going to fuck my ass or keep talking?"

She narrows her eyes, accepting my response for what it is—a challenge. Holding my stare, she pulls the vibrator almost all the way out and slams it back in me again. It still hurts like a mother, but the pleasure is also insane. This is exactly the kind of shit I love.

"Are you enjoying yourself?" she asks, not as sweetly as before.

"Fuck yeah," I groan.

"Good."

She keeps the dildo plunged deep in my ass and presses the switchblade into my skin between my shoulder blades, going deep. I clench my jaw, and yet, a grunt escapes my throat. The pain from the knife cutting into me, mixed with the pleasurable burn from the dildo, is making me delirious and horny as fuck. My balls are tight, but there isn't enough friction around my cock, and I need it desperately, so I begin to fuck the mattress, for lack of a better word.

"If you keep moving, your tattoo will be all messed up."

"I don't care."

She keeps pressing the blade into my skin, and if I were to guess, she's writing her name in cursive because Valerie would be extra like that. But I soon become too lost in all the sensations competing for attention. The sharp sting of the blade slicing my skin, the blood trickling down my back, and that damn dildo vibrating in my ass.

I begin to grind my hips hard against the mattress,

chasing the orgasm that seems close and yet so far away. My eyes are closed, and sweat has covered my skin. It feels as if I'll die if I don't find release soon.

The pressure from the blade disappears, and a second later, Valerie whispers in my ear, "How badly do you want to come, babe?"

I open my eyes to glower at her, but my retort is swallowed by her tongue in my mouth. She holds my chin, keeping my head at an awkward angle and I forget what I was going to say. Instead, I cherish the savagery of her hard kiss. I bite her lower lip and tug when she pulls away.

There's a bit of blood on my tongue now. "You taste delicious, kitty cat."

She wipes the blood off with a finger and grins. "I want to taste you too."

Shiiit. Knowing her, I can expect a few bites myself. She rolls me onto my side, and that forces my arms into an odd and uncomfortable angle. But I don't complain when she wraps her luscious mouth around my cock and takes me out of my misery.

"Fuuck!" She barely has to do a thing before I'm coming in her mouth. I was already too worked up. "That's it, kitty cat. You suck me so good."

She plays with my balls as my cock throbs in her mouth. The orgasm seems to last longer than normal, probably because of the vibrator giving me an extra boost of pleasure.

Valerie only stops sucking me when my body goes slack, and I let out a sigh of contentment. My eyes are closed when she pulls back, and I'm sure I'm sporting the goofiest grin.

A moment later, the cuffs click open, but Valerie is walking away.

"Kitty cat? Where are you going?"

"Don't move just yet." She disappears into the bathroom and walks out a couple seconds later, holding a bottle in her hand.

"What's that?"

"The grand finale. Back on your stomach."

I return to my original position, but now that my arms are no longer bound to the headboard and I just had the best orgasm of my life, I'm relaxed as fuck, even though the dildo is still fucking me.

That lasts only a few seconds more, and then Valerie douses my back with something that feels like acid.

"Motherfucker!" I jerk, but Valerie is sitting on the backs of my legs, and I can't move far.

"Don't be such a baby. It's just an antiseptic solution."

"Are you sure? It feels like you mixed it with hot sauce."

She laughs, turning me into a pool of mush again. Her laughter is my biggest weakness. "I can't believe I didn't think of that. Next time."

Free to move, I roll onto my side and push Valerie off my legs. She falls onto the mattress next to me, and I don't waste time before I'm on top of her and between her legs with my cock ready for round two.

"Woof. I didn't think you'd recover so fast," she says.

"What can I say? It's this damn sex toy in my ass. You've woken a beast, kitty cat." I finally pull the dildo out 'cause it's done its job.

"A beast that's now properly branded with my name."

"I'll always belong to you, with or without your name carved into my skin."

Her eyes go soft, which is a rare thing to witness when it comes to Valerie. She's a feral black cat, through and through. "I'm yours too, Eric, in this lifetime and the next."

I laugh, remembering she said the exact opposite a year ago. "I'll always find you, kitty cat. No matter what. You're mine."

THE END

🔪🔪🔪

Thank you so much for reading Valerie and Eric's story. I hope you enjoyed it. Please consider leaving a review.

If you want more dark romance stories featuring unhinged heroes , I recommend my FILTHY GODS series.

Start with *Falling for Catastrophe.* **ONE-CLICK NOW.**

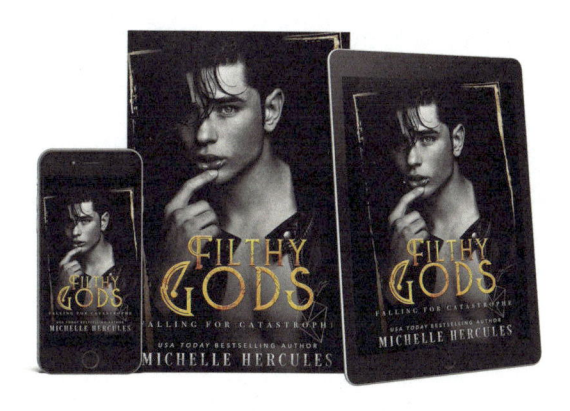

Three years ago, I fell in love with a monster. I barely

survived, and now I've been given a second chance at Maverick Prep.

My plan was to keep my head down and not draw attention to myself.

Then Jason Novak came into my life like a thunderstorm.

Furious.
Devastating.
Loud.

The devil incarnate, he has a reputation for cruelty that precedes him. Not even his angelic face can hide his black heart.

He wants something I've earned fair and square, and now he hates me.

My survival instincts are telling me to flee. But I've already let a monster take too much from me once. My name. My dreams. My home. I won't let another asshole do that to me again.

Standing up to Jason becomes a dangerous game.

There's a fine line between love and hate, and we're about to obliterate it.

If you like morally gray characters, psychotic heroes, and badass heroines this is for you. This story contains dark themes that may be triggering to some readers.

ONE-CLICK NOW!

about the author

USA Today Bestselling Author Michelle Hercules always knew creative arts were her calling but not in a million years did she think she would become an author. With a background in fashion design she thought she would follow that path. But one day, out of the blue, she had an idea for a book. One page turned into ten pages, ten pages turned into a hundred, and before she knew it, her first novel, The Prophecy of Arcadia, was born.

Michelle Hercules resides in Florida with her husband and daughter. She is currently working on the *Blueblood Vampires* series and the *Filthy Gods* series.

Sign-up for Michelle Hercules' Newsletter:
bit.ly/MichelleHerculesVIP

Join Michelle Hercules' Readers Group:

https://www.facebook.com/groups/mhsoars

🔪🔪🔪

Connect with Michelle Hercules:

www.michellehercules.com

books@mhsoars.com

- facebook.com/michelleherculesauthor
- instagram.com/michelleherculesauthor
- amazon.com/Michelle-Hercules/e/B075652M8M
- bookbub.com/authors/michelle-hercules
- tiktok.com/@michelleherculesauthor?
- youtube.com/@MichelleHerculesAuthor
- patreon.com/michellehercules

Made in the USA
Columbia, SC
15 November 2024